Angel

HELEN CAVANAGH

SCHOLASTIC INC.
New York Toronto London Auckland Sydney

For my son Larry:

Once an angel face,
always an angel face.

With Love

ISBN 0-590-32284-2

12 11 10 9 8 7 6 5 4 3   6 7 8/8

Printed in the U.S.A.   01

Angel

A Wildfire Book

One

It was almost noon on a clear October Saturday and Angel Porter was already tired. Discouraged, too, and so lonesome she felt like crying.

Angel had walked to the mall alone, arriving just as the doors opened, and spent two hours trudging in and out of stores looking for something to buy. Nothing appealed to her, and she thought it was because she really didn't want to shop. Walking, she had tried hard to keep her head high and a happy, interested expression on her face. But it was a big waste of time. Angel was sick of it, sick of herself.

Not that she didn't have lots of time to waste. That was the problem. Her best friends from Edgemont High, Jody Farringer and Tania James, had gone away for the weekend and Angel missed them. Earlier that morning, sitting in her mother's spotless, too-quiet kitchen, Angel decided that she couldn't just sit around all day. The mile-and-a-half walk to the Birch Tree Mall was an excellent thing to do on such a lovely day. She could spend the last of her birthday money and also a few of the hours that loomed ahead of her. The weekend would be endless unless she did something. She could work on her project of redecorating and building furniture for her room.

She usually loved working on the project. It filled her with pride and satisfaction to look at the arrangement of shelves covering one wall, knowing that she had cut, sanded, stained, and varnished each piece of wood. The platform bed — her masterpiece — was sanded and ready to stain, but Angel had decided to let it go for today. She felt like being with people, even strangers.

Angel savored the long walk to the mall. She didn't envy the joggers who passed her, sweating, panting, and staring straight ahead. She preferred her own slower pace because she could look at the bright blue sky and the trees that were bursting into red, gold, and orange flames. Angel loved autumn, when everything was so colorful and the air so cool and fragrant.

Walking took her mind off her feelings of anger and frustration. She wouldn't have to be so bored right now if she could go away for the weekend with her family like Jody, or meet her boyfriend in Staten Island like Tania. *Well, I can't really be jealous of Tania,* Angel thought. *I'm so shy around boys that they think I'm stuck up and stay away from me. And as for going away for a weekend with my parents*, Angel sighed to herself, *forget about that. They don't even know I exist. Even if they could ever tear themselves away from their work for one weekend it wouldn't be to take me anywhere.* Angel guessed that she must bore them. That was why she had started telling them "stories" after all. *Don't call them "stories,"* Angel said to herself in disgust. *They're lies pure and simple and they're starting to get out of hand.*

She'd tried so hard to entertain her parents during her years of growing up. She yearned for them to pay attention, to acknowledge that she was important. When she told the stories . . . the lies . . . they seemed to sit up and take notice. That's all the lies had been at first — harmless stories, make-believe, imagination, and as much drama as she could give them. Angel worried that they were starting to get out of hand.

The only other times they seemed to notice and enjoy her was when she had done something new and becoming with her hair, or when she modeled a new outfit for them, or when she tried new makeup techniques.

They liked showing her off to visitors and friends, too. If someone raved about Angel to her parents, they would look at each other with the same kind of satisfaction they showed when someone admired their apricot wall-to-wall carpeting, or the new glass and brass etagere in the foyer. They adored re-

ceiving compliments on all their pretty things
— furniture, paintings, their few pieces of
sculpture — and Angel.

Her parents liked having a pretty, orna-
mental daughter to show off. How many times
had her mother jokingly remarked about
Angel's special coloring — the rose-tawny
skin, the soft, light brown hair and clear
blue eyes. Mom's favorite color scheme was
apricot, cream, gold, and blue. A few times
Angel had wondered if she was adopted. It
was hard to believe that her parents had
been lucky enough to have a child born to
them who so exactly matched the decor.

Angel poked around the mall for two
hours, stopping in one store after another.
She wasn't finding anything she liked, but
she wasn't ready to go home. Her birthday
money was still in the back pocket of her
jeans. Angel had folded the two crisp ten-
dollar bills into a fat square, and she patted
it, wondering if she should spend some of it
for food. Except for juice and one slice of
toast that morning, she'd eaten nothing since
six o'clock the night before. Angel decided
that lunch would be part of her birthday
present and a reward for making it through
the morning.

Heading toward the opposite end of the
mall, Angel felt slightly better. Just having
something to do, a destination, helped.

At Hot Sam's she ordered a medium Coke
and a fat, hot pretzel with cheese. Just looking at the rich brown twist of dough drip-

ping with gooey cheese cheered her up. Turning, with the container of Coke in one hand, the pretzel in the other, Angel spotted an empty space on one of the benches. There was a man sitting on the bench, but his back was to her. Angel sat down, took a sip of Coke, and set it down beside her. She bit into the pretzel and immediately regretted it. The cheese oozed like orange-yellow lava down her chin and onto her best blue sweater. Angel could feel the heat of it, but for a second or two she didn't move, didn't even look down at the mess.

Just what I need, she thought dismally. *The finishing touch, the last straw. What do I do now?* Angel had remembered to take a straw from the counter, but not napkins. If Tania and Jody were here with her, it would have been funny, something to laugh together about. No big deal. But it wasn't funny now. Tears of humiliation and depression were welling up in her eyes.

"Here, sweetheart, don't cry. Use this before it stains."

Startled, Angel looked into the warm, sympathetic brown eyes of a moon-faced, bald man who was waving a large white handkerchief under her nose. He had swiveled around so that he was facing her.

When she looked down at her sweater and at the pretzel, she saw that strands of cheese were continuing to drip, from hand to sweater, and a glob was on her jeans, too.

"Such a shame," the man said kindly. "A

pretty sweater and an even prettier girl wearing it. Here — take it."

His eyes were echoing the compliment, and all at once, his admiration and his interference were too much.

"No, thanks," she said coldly. "I'll get some napkins." She got up and, remembering her Coke, bent to pick it up with her free hand. The man wasn't smiling at her anymore. "Thanks, anyway," she managed grudgingly.

Angel wished that he had minded his own business. She hurried back to the counter and the girl took one look and nodded knowingly.

"Happens a lot," she said. "Good thing you didn't order the *pizza* and cheese." She handed Angel a stack of napkins. "Delicious but disastrous, if you know what I mean."

Now I know, Angel thought, as she mopped up the worst of the mess. It still felt sticky although most of the cheese was gone. The girl handed her a handful of napkins that she had dampened. "Here. Maybe it's not ruined. I love your sweater . . . such a pretty color."

At least she wasn't going to hear about how pretty *she* was; girls usually didn't say that to each other. Because if she heard it one more time she was going to scream.

"Are you a model or something?" The girl was leaning on the counter, her chin in her hands, and Angel took one look at her wistful, slightly envious expression, and left, not

6

bothering to answer the boringly familiar question.

Angel found an empty bench, and sat down. With napkins surrounding all but a small portion of the pretzel, she ate it and finished her Coke. Surprisingly, quite a bit of cheese remained on the pretzel. It wasn't hot enough but she ate it. Even though she wasn't hungry anymore, she was still restless and reluctant to go home.

After she put her garbage into a trash receptacle, Angel spotted a small stand that she'd missed, *The Silver Connection,* and headed for it eagerly. Angel thought she might find something to buy there . . . maybe a sterling chain, or another charm to add to the charm bracelet she'd gotten as a birthday gift. She'd wanted one for ages, and even though the fad had died a while ago, Angel was pleased on her birthday when she opened the narrow silver box and saw the elegant silver bracelet. "Oh, thanks, Mom . . . Dad. I love it. Just what I wanted."

She loved it until she studied the charms that her parents had chosen, and the two from her cousins, and realized for the two-hundredth time that they didn't know her at all. The six charms must be jokes, she thought. All of them represented how others saw her — sweet, pretty, dainty, almost perfect. Her cousins had given her a fragile little butterfly and a miniature, long-stemmed rose. Mom and Dad had chosen the expected sweet sixteen charm, and another one, which they meant to be funny, which said, "90% Angel."

Tania had commemorated their shared stint on the track team during freshman and sophomore years with a whimsical little roadrunner. Jody, who lived and breathed theater and wanted all her friends to do the same, gave Angel a tiny tragedy-and-comedy mask. Her friends, at least, recognized that she was a real person with real interests.

Angel approached the booth and spotted the charms right away, dozens of them, each nestled on a bed of black velvet. She was glad that the saleswoman wasn't the pushy, too-helpful type. She was sweet-faced, quite old, with blue-gray hair, and glasses dangling from a chain around her neck. She smiled at Angel and said that she would be ready and happy to help her if she saw something she liked. "Just holler, dear." Angel laughed politely at the woman's joke, but she could have been serious because when she put on her glasses and began to separate a large tangle of chains, she did seem oblivious to everything.

One by one, Angel scanned the charms, noting a few of the price tags, and saw that they were within her range. The tiny telephone was cute but she really wasn't a phone person like some of the kids she knew, and like the silver unicorn and the darling little mushroom, it had no meaning for her. The piano charm was out of the question, she decided. She'd had lessons from third grade until seventh and had never made it past hopeless.

One section was all hearts, big ones the size of a quarter, and tiny ones, flat and rounded, etched and plain. Angel especially liked the heart with a key attached to it, but she was aware that a heart wasn't something you bought for yourself. Someday, when she had a boyfriend, he might buy one for her as a Valentine's gift.

Up and down the rows, Angel searched and paused and considered. Nothing at *The Silver Connection* was connecting at all. She couldn't seem to find the right charm to represent the real Angela Marie Porter, or, rather, that *other* Angel no one else knew existed. She didn't know what she was looking for, but she was sure that she would know it on sight.

Not a tennis racquet, not rollerskates, not the tiny comb, or the little silver ballet slipper. Not right, any of them.

Embarrassed because she was taking so long, Angel looked up, but the woman wasn't paying attention to anything except the chains that she was arranging so carefully on a velvet pad. Bending closer to see the details of the small charms, Angel's nose almost made contact with the glass and her soft brown hair slid silkily forward to shield her face from the gaze of passing shoppers. Not being able to see anything but the charms helped, because Angel suddenly spotted one that she couldn't remember seeing before.

A connection. Finally. It was so perfect that for a minute Angel couldn't believe it. Not only could this tiny Pinocchio be passed off as a symbol for her hobby, but it would stand for the *other* Angel. The charm could be a talisman, like a string tied around a finger, a reminder, something to help her stop telling little lies — it was getting to be a habit.

Who would ever guess that the storybook puppet and Angel Porter had something in common, or that they were kindred spirits, maybe even twins?

The only difference between me and Pinocchio, she thought, *is that my nose doesn't give me away.*

Angel called softly to the saleswoman. It wasn't a joke after all; she had to call twice more. "Could I see that one, please?" she asked, pointing.

The woman set her work aside, and for safekeeping put it beneath a counter in the center of her booth. She slid back a panel at the back of the glass case, and reaching in, picked up a charm. "Oh, yes," the woman said, smiling tenderly. "Exactly. It suits you, dear."

"*No,*" Angel said firmly. "Not the ballerina. Pinocchio."

The blue-haired woman looked startled, then faintly disapproving. "*Pinocchio?*"

"How much?" Angel asked calmly, and added before the woman answered, "I'll take it."

"Twelve dollars and tax." She replaced the ballerina and picked up Pinocchio gingerly. Watching, Angel sighed. She knew why the woman was displeased; it had happened lots of times before. Angel had learned that some people got upset if she didn't live up to her image. She looked like an angel — blue eyes, heart-shaped face, dimples, and soft hair — her name was Angel, so, it followed, she was supposed to be angelic. Whatever that was . . . she'd never been sure.

"Thank you," the woman said as she took Angel's money and the charm and walked to the register. "I'll put it in a little box for you."

Waiting, Angel suddenly wondered what Great Aunt Elizabeth would think if she knew what her grand-niece had bought with the money she'd sent for her birthday. Not just what, but why. The gentle woman would never believe in a million years that her darling Angel was anything but wonderful and perfect and good.

A month ago, her great aunt invited Angel to be her guest of honor at her art show at the Lars Graversen Gallery in New Brunswick, New Jersey. In New Brunswick, Elizabeth Emma Clavell was considered a city treasure.

The day was supposed to be a birthday surprise — the show, followed by an elegant lunch at the new Hyatt Hotel. Angel was very proud of her locally famous relative but she had a few bad moments when she came

11

face-to-face with an entire wall of "Angel" portraits. She hadn't dreamed that the charcoal sketches her great aunt had done of her during her last visit would be the basis for her new show. "Angels" large and small, framed and unframed, were all sold within an hour of the show's opening. Art lovers seemed to adore the soft-edged, highly romantic pastel portraits, and they also loved it that the artist's model was there in person. One woman even asked for Angel's autograph!

Great Aunt Elizabeth gave Angel one of the larger portraits, and it hung now in the living room above the fireplace. For weeks her parents ooohed and ahhhed, and showed it to anyone who came into the house.

"Here you are," the saleswoman said. "I could have sworn you were a dancer or something like that."

"I'm a carpenter," Angel said icily. "The man who made Pinocchio was a wood-carver, remember? I don't make puppets though — mostly furniture." Angel couldn't stop. "I build sets for drama club. I help with the lighting, too, and the props." She showed her teeth in fake smile. "Dirty jobs, but *someone* has to do them."

The woman's reaction was just what she hoped. "Oh . . . my! How very . . . ah . . . interesting!"

She left the woman standing with her mouth open and her eyes bulging. Angel deliberately walked jauntily, swinging the little silver bag, and she thought if anyone was watching her they would have to think she was in a carefree mood. The fact was that her mood zigzagged between anger and depression, those feelings fighting with each other and causing an uproar in her mind. When she found a place to sit on a round bench, depression won.

It wasn't fair, she thought, but people would probably keep on making their stupid snap judgments, and she would have to put up with it, or like just now, find a way to protest.

No one even considered the possibility that she might not be so pretty and perfect inside. They looked at Angel and all they seemed to see was hair and eye color, skin tone and features. She wasn't overly tall or too short, not fat and not too thin. Nothing outside to detract from the portrait of an angelically pretty girl.

It was the same old story, and finally Angel decided that she just couldn't keep going over it. She took the little silvery box from the paper bag, then lifted the cover. There, under a layer of cotton, Pinocchio gleamed — two tiny silver eyes above a needle-nose. He wore a hat, suspenders, short pants, and an aura of slyness. Angel decided that she would put him next to the ninety percent Angel charm, and let him stand for the other ten percent.

Her feet hurt. She wasn't going to make it home on foot. Angel sat for a while longer, then decided to call home for a ride. Mom and Dad ("The Siamese Twins," as Angel had nicknamed them) would drive up to the mall together, for they were rarely apart on weekends and evenings. Angel would feel like excess baggage in the back seat as she always did when she rode in the car with them. She hoped they would bother to answer the phone, she thought, as she dropped a coin into the slot on the pay phone.

Her father did. "Jack Porter here."

It made her laugh when her father did his English gentleman bit. "Angel Porter *here*," she said, chuckling.

There was a long pause in which her father did not laugh. Finally, he asked: "*Where* is here? I thought you were in bed."

Her smile disappeared. She heard the irritation in his voice but that didn't hurt half as much as the fact that her parents hadn't even checked to see if she was in her room, or called her down for breakfast.

"Your mother and I have been up since ten, and we've been tip-toeing around here all this time so we wouldn't wake you."

Scowling at the phone in her hand, she apologized, although the only thing she was truly sorry about was that she had to bother them at all. "I'm at the mall. I walked up, but I've been wandering around since it opened and I'm beat. Could you please pick me up?"

"Oh, *Angel*. Of all times. We've just made a fresh pot of coffee and I have the plans for the new store spread out on the table. Your mother was just about to take a look. It really *is* a very inconvenient time. How about having one of your friends' parents pick you up this time?"

"Dad, I'm alone. My friends are away this weekend. That's why I came here — for something to do."

She heard the deep sigh, then muffled words and she knew her parents were having a conference. Finally, her father said, "All right, Angel. Be sure and wait out front so I can see you. I don't want to waste time today."

Angel managed a choked "good-bye" and hung up. Slowly, she replaced the receiver and then walked toward the main entrance, ignoring the group of boys trailing behind her, and their coaxing remarks: "Hey, beautiful. Can't you say hello?" and "Smile pretty for the camera, gorgeous."

Outside, she leaned against a pillar, lifted her face to the sky, and closed her eyes. The sun was directly overhead, and it warmed her skin and scalp, but inside Angel felt cold, sad, and alone. She thought of Jody up at the cabin in the mountains laughing and learning her lines with her mother and Aunt Mary. She had been picked for the female lead in the play. Her friend was so conscientious; Angel was sure that by the end of the weekend Jody would know all her lines by heart. *Grease*, they'd all agreed, was going to be the most fun of any play they'd ever done. Tania was going to be Frenchy, but she wasn't worrying about her lines yet, Angel knew. Staten Island and a boy named Bobby Daniels took first place this weekend.

She spotted her father's black Buick turning into the parking lot entrance, and went over to the curb to wait. She pasted a smile on her mouth and waved. "Here I am, Dad."

Riding home Angel decided that just as soon as she got home she was going to go straight to her room and work on the platform bed. Maybe by Sunday night it would be finished, and she could start on the end tables. Maybe like the scent of clean, new wood, her bad feelings would rise from her mind and escape through her open window. Working on her project would make time drift away, too.

Angel stole a glance at her father. He sat frowning and silent behind the wheel. She knew he wasn't happy about picking her up, but it wouldn't have killed him to talk a little, Angel thought. It would have been nice if he would at least pretend that she was something more than a nuisance.

Looking out the window as the car sped toward home, Angel's eyes felt itchy, then moist. But what was there to cry about? She knew that her parents weren't going to change. They were too wrapped up in their work to notice Angel, let alone try to understand her. Her parents both still worked for Harvest Foods, a grocery store chain, where they had met twenty years ago. Mom was now the assistant director of advertising and it was her job to write the appealing radio, TV, and newspaper announcements that brought hordes of shoppers into Harvest Foods. Dad was operations manager. Mom and Dad were both important employees but Angel wondered why Mom wanted to do most of her work at home when her "other half" was out in the field. As far as Angel was concerned, both parents were out very far in the field.

T*wo*

About eight o'clock on Sunday night Jody called Angel and laughingly bragged that she'd not only learned her lines but "Danny's," too. Danny Zuko, the leader of the Thunderbirds, was the role John Travolta played in the movie version of *Grease*. Although Jody already had the part of Sandy, Danny's girl friend, his part hadn't been filled yet. Jody said that none of the boys who tried out had even come close, and the drama coach, Mr. Damian, was getting nervous.

An hour later, Tania called and spent fifteen minutes raving about how wonderful her third date with Bobby Daniels had been. At least three times during the conversation, Tania told Angel that Bobby was brilliant, funny, and great looking. He had taken her out to dinner at an Italian restaurant.

"Candlelight. And, oh, Angel, he read my palm." She giggled. "He saw a tall, dark, handsome stranger in my future."

"*Bobby* is tall, dark, and handsome," Angel said, laughing.

Tania let out a loud breath. "Yes, but he's not a stranger, Angel. Not anymore. Bobby kissed me twice last night. He's *so* sweet."

Angel was truly happy for Tania. It was a shame, though, that she had to travel all the way to Staten Island to see a boyfriend. Bobby was the son of a good friend of Tania's father. Tania's father *said* that he didn't really mind driving to the island on weekends because it gave him a chance to visit with old friends, but Angel didn't think that was going to last forever. Why couldn't Bobby drive to Edgemont to see Tania? Still, it couldn't be easy to be the only black girl in town. Except for one other family who had three sons already out of college and married, Tania and her family were the exception in all-white Edgemont. Tania never complained — or at least, not much — but Angel knew she suffered sometimes. She wondered how she would feel if the situation were reversed.

When she finished talking with Tania, Angel wandered into the den and saw that her parents were totally engrossed in an old English movie, so she said good-night and went upstairs to bed. She didn't even make an effort to pick out the clothes she wanted to wear on Monday morning, or bother opening the novel that she was reading. Feeling depressed as well as tired, she fell asleep almost immediately.

The next day was Monday and Angel looked forward to school. At least someone there would know she was alive.

At noon after fourth period English, she headed for the cafeteria. She had stayed after class to sign out a copy of *Catcher in the Rye*, which Mr. Douglas had assigned. He'd warned that he was going to give a quiz in exactly a week. The hallway was deserted, and Angel walked slowly, flipping the pages of the paperback, reading a paragraph here and there, and smiling at some of the dialogue. Holden Caulfield already intrigued her. He was funny and. . . .

"On your way to lunch, Angel?"

She whirled sharply, bumping her nose and chin against a warm and solid green-striped shirt. She hadn't heard anyone behind her.

"Whoa — easy. It's only me. I didn't mean to sneak up on you, Angel. I really scared you. Are you okay?"

Angel stepped back and looked up. Over the summer Jay Butler had to have grown at least four inches. He was so tall now, and very lanky, she thought. He was grinning at her, but Angel saw concern in his hazel eyes. For as long as she'd known him, Jay's usual expression was faintly worried, and he rarely smiled.

"I'm okay. Guess I was really caught up in this." She held up the book. Her shoulders still tingled from the warmth and weight of his hands when he had reached out to steady her.

"But you *are* on your way to lunch, right?"

He was staring at her; she could feel his intense gaze without even turning her head. She kept walking, raising her chin slightly and staring straight ahead. It made her feel uncomfortable, knowing that he was looking at her. "You're gorgeous, Angel. I've always thought so."

"Thanks," she said, still not looking at him. She could feel a burning sensation in her cheeks, but she knew that her blush never showed on the outside. She was grateful for the kind of skin that wasn't an instant give-away, like Jody's petal pink and white complexion. Angel had been looking at Jay Butler in a brand new way since the beginning of school this year, and now he was spoiling it. Too bad, she thought grimly, that he has to act just like all the rest.

She stopped walking abruptly. Jay stopped, too, and looked at her questioningly. "What's the matter? Forget something?"

"Yes," she answered, deliberately not meeting his eyes. "I did forget. I'm not eating lunch today. I'm on a three-day fast."

When his eyes widened and his jaw dropped slightly, Angel realized what she had done. Too late, her hand sought her talisman. Pinocchio couldn't help her now. Like so many of her lies, this one had no reason and no warning. The words had just slipped out without any thought or effort.

Jay burst out laughing. "Are you kidding? What for? You certainly don't need to lose weight. You're perfect just the way you are."

He shook his head. "A *fast*? That's crazy, Angel."

He doesn't know how right he is, Angel thought grimly. Crazy was exactly what she'd thought of the article in *Best Self* magazine. To Angel the thought of going even one day without food seemed not only crazy, but impossible. She couldn't admit that to Jay, though.

"It's not crazy, Jay. Fasting cleanses the body, rids it of all kinds of harmful chemicals. Occasionally, the body needs to . . ." What was she saying? She was spouting what she'd read and it was strange, because she hadn't even thought that the article had anything to do with her. ". . . purify itself. My Dad works for Harvest Foods, and you should hear some of the stories he tells about the stuff that's in meat, for instance. Most of the foods we eat are crammed with additives and preservatives. If we would only pay attention to labels. . . ."

"I guess," Jay said without interest. "But I don't think I want to hear about it, or I'll lose my appetite. Come on, Angel, forget the fast. You're going to get sick if you don't eat. How far into the fast are you, anyway?"

"The third day," Angel said, then panicked. Her mind raced to remember if Jody and Tania had seen her eat anything. She relaxed when she realized that she hadn't been with either of them since Friday evening. No one except her parents and, of course, strangers at the mall, had seen her eat all weekend. She was safe.

Not really, though, she thought. She'd fixed it so that she couldn't go into the cafeteria unless she followed Jay's advice and ate something. She was really hungry, which was one reason she was furious with herself. Jay would sit with her, and he'd mention her fast to Jody and Tania, and they would question her, and, probably tease her. She didn't think she would be able to handle it, especially since the food smells wafting through the open cafeteria door were already making her mouth water and her stomach growl. She had really messed up this time. But she couldn't admit that she wasn't on a fast, or even pretend to give in to her hunger. Either way Jay would think she wasn't a serious person, someone who could make up her mind and stick to a decision.

"I'll see you later, Jay. I'm going to sit outside and read some of this book. I'm really not hungry at all. They say that's what happens after you've gone without food for a while. But you have a nice lunch."

She smiled in his general direction and then turned and walked very fast toward the big double doors. *Have a nice lunch — what a joke*, she thought, pushing at the heavy door.

Except it wasn't a joke anymore. She hated herself for this latest, dumb lie. What was the sense of it? There was no sense. The fact was, she was hopeless, a real case.

"Hey, Angel. Wait a sec."

Jay hurried toward her, and she let the door swing shut as she waited for him. *What now?* she wondered. *If he tries to persuade me to come to lunch again, I won't be able to resist.*

"After school —" Angel saw that he was slightly flustered, and she softened toward him. She allowed him a small, encouraging smile. "After school, what?"

"Wait for me, okay? We can talk. Maybe, over a slice of pizza and a Coke?"

"You're forgetting my fast," Angel said, turning away.

"Oh, yeah," Jay said. She couldn't see the expression on his face, but she heard the disappointment in his voice. She hadn't planned to say it, but afterward, she was glad she had. "Wait a minute, Jay. We get out at two-thirty? I forgot — my fast is over at exactly two o'clock. I'd love a slice and a Coke. I'll meet you out front."

She turned and looked at Jay just in time to see his bright smile.

"Good," he said, and made a gesture that was half wave, half victory sign. Angel went outside and sat down on the broad top step. She opened the paperback and forced herself to read the entire first chapter. Then she closed the book and turned her face up to the sun, and thought about Jay. She did want to get to know him better, but she wondered if she could ever have as close a friendship with him as Jody did.

Jay lived on Jody's street, three houses

away. They'd been friends and neighbors since kindergarten. Jody had always had good things to say about him, even when he was so shy that he couldn't even say hi without getting red in the face. Jody had told Angel that Jay had a hard time opening up with most people, but Angel knew that he was very comfortable with her. Angel hadn't been too interested then, but she remembered now that Jody had described Jay as a "quality guy" with a good sense of humor when you got to know him. When school had started in September, Jody had nudged her as they were walking to class one day. Jay was walking toward them and he smiled and waved at Jody, and kept going.

"Did you notice how tall he is now, Angel? And how cute? If he wasn't like a brother to me, I might get ideas. How about you, Angel?"

Angel hadn't answered that question. Instead, she said irritably, "Looks aren't everything, Jody."

Jody had just laughed. "They don't *hurt*."

Angel wondered what Jody would say when she told her that she was going to meet Jay after school. There wasn't any problem, since it was true that Jody and Jay were just friends, Angel thought. She was sure that Jody would be glad for her, and for Jay. She sighed. Not only would she have to starve until two-thirty, but she had also missed having lunch and talking with Jody and Tania.

With time to spare before the bell, Angel went back into school and walked to the nearest girls' room. She took her time brushing her hair, and freshening her blush and lipstick. When she was through, Angel stepped back and looked at herself in the mirror for several seconds, then — abruptly — stuck out her tongue at herself.

She turned and walked out of the girls' room thinking that the mirror lied, too. It only showed the outside — skin, hair, eyes, teeth — perfect, unblemished. An apple could look perfect, too, she thought, but when you bit into the smooth, rosy skin, there could be a soft, rotten spot, that made you feel sick and disgusted. *You throw rotten apples in the garbage, right? Well, I have a rotten spot, too,* she thought, *and if anyone knew, they'd be disgusted, sickened. I'd get thrown away fast.*

She met Jody in the hall, and Angel quickly hid her troubles beneath a smile.

"Where were you? How come you didn't show up for lunch? I missed you. Tania did, too. We haven't seen you all weekend."

Angel ignored Jody's question about lunch because she didn't want to continue the lie about her fast. She blurted out the news about Jay, and, as she'd hoped, it distracted Jody.

"That's great," Jody said, in her warm, bubbly voice. Her voice matched her personality, Angel had always thought. "And you're not excited?" Jody rolled her eyes. "This is a first, kid."

"I'm a late-bloomer, I guess," Angel said, happier now, because of Jody's enthusiasm.

"I really don't know why," Jody said, more seriously. "You're fantastic, Angel — the prettiest girl at Edgemont High, forget just the junior class."

"Hmmm," was all that Angel could manage. Jody wasn't pretty, at least, not as far as features were concerned. Her nose was too long, and her mouth too wide. Her brown curly hair had a mind of its own, and she was tall and kind of boney. But most people saw Jody as pretty. She had a sort of glow about her, a magnetic quality that drew people close. Tania and Angel had analyzed why people were always attracted to her. They'd decided it was because Jody had more energy than most people, and that because she really cared about people, they cared about her.

They had almost reached history class, but Jody put a hand on Angel's arm. "Listen, do me a favor. See if you can convince Jay to try out for Danny's part. I've almost talked him into it, and I promised to coach him, but you know Jay, he has so many doubts about himself. He's helped me with my lines often enough — played the male lead enough times in my family room. He's good, Angel. He can act."

Angel looked at Jody. "Why would he listen to me?"

"You're the expert, Angel. I mean, behind-the-scenes, and an all around helpful person." Jody wrinkled her nose. "But if you think I'm going to stand here and list your talents, you are wrong. We're going to be late for class. Just do it, Angel. Get Jay to want to play Danny. Tell him you'll coach him every day after school and on weekends." Jody shot Angel a mischievous look. "If I know Jay, it will work like magic. I know he likes you and thinks you're pretty."

Angel didn't answer, because she wasn't sure yet that she wanted to have Jay around all the time, especially if he was interested in her only because he thought she was pretty. Angel wasn't interested in a boy-friend under those conditions.

She wasn't in a very good mood during history, and she felt worse in art class. Angel was grateful that her collage required quiet concentration and the cutting and pasting helped keep her mind off her problems, but she wasn't entirely successful.

It was hard not to think about her most recent lie. Her growling stomach wasn't letting her forget it.

Three

As she waited for Jay after school, Angel sat on the same broad step she had sat on at lunch. The first rush from the double doors was over, and only a few kids lingered on the walkway, talking and fooling around in groups of two and three. It was a beautiful day, like summer, and again Angel tipped her head back to catch the waning rays of sun.

Tania and Jody had stopped to talk to her, but only briefly. Tania was happy about Angel going out with Jay, even if it was only for pizza in the afternoon.

"Have fun," they chorused and hurried away. Tania turned when she was halfway down the walk and shouted, "Pick you up for rehearsal, Angel."

At that moment, the door opened and Jay came out, glowering. He walked over and sat down beside her, and shook his head disgustedly.

"Sorry I'm late, Angel. I had to stop by

the office. I was paged over the intercom last period. I *hate* that."

Jay was frowning ferociously now. She felt a sudden impulse to reach over and smooth out the deep furrows in his forehead.

"I didn't hear it. Of course, that's because Mr. Martino turns off the p.a. system. He has a thing about unnecessary noise when artists are at work. Hey, why did they want you, Jay? Are you in trouble or something?" She couldn't imagine it.

"No big deal. They just wanted to bug me about being late so much. Mrs. Thompson insisted that I have to have a written excuse from home. She made me feel like an eight-year-old."

Angel wished that he would snap out of this bad mood. It was beginning to make her nervous. She tried to joke him out of it.

"What's the matter, Lazybones? Can't get out of bed in the morning? Tell me, how many times does your mother have to call you before you finally get up?"

His sharp, probing look surprised her. Now he seemed mad at *her*. Then the storm on his face cleared.

"Yeah, right. I should get up earlier. I'm going to work on it." He stood up and she followed his example. He stood one step above her, and he seemed impossibly tall. Angel felt herself relax.

"How about that pizza?" she asked lightly. "My fast is over and I want to celebrate."

She felt Jay's hand on her elbow as he

guided her down the steps. "Sounds good to me," he said softly. "Let's hurry before you die from starvation."

Archer's Deli served hamburgers, subs hot and cold, and the best pizza for miles around. It was just two blocks away from Edgemont High, and usually it was packed after school. Not that day; Angel was surprised to find the place almost empty. George and Flo, the middle-aged couple who owned the place, greeted Angel warmly and smiled at Jay. Angel, Jody, and Tania came to the deli often, and the couple treated them like family.

Jay left Angel in the booth and went to put in their order. He'd told her he intended to buy a small pie instead of just two slices. "I plan to keep you here for a while, and I know you're hungry. I can see it in your eyes."

He is nice, Angel thought, *and for the moment anyway, he is thinking of my insides. One point for him,* she thought, settling into the worn, wooden booth.

Angel was grateful when the pizza and Cokes arrived, and also because Jay didn't expect her to make conversation. They put first things first, and for Jay as well as Angel, the top priority was food.

"I've been eating like crazy lately," he admitted, dropping a last crust of pizza on the empty tray. "All summer, too. I grew this way —" He pointed upward. He stretched his arms out sideways. "— but not this way."

"I look like a telephone pole or something."

Angel was surprised that he sounded self-conscious about his new height. She would have thought he'd be proud.

"Jody was saving you a seat at lunch, you know. She almost flipped when I told her you'd been fasting for three days. She said, and I quote: 'That crazy Angel. What is she doing that for?'"

Angel sighed with relief. If Jody hadn't been away all weekend, she would have been proved a liar.

Jay was leaning back, and because there wasn't enough room under the booth for his long legs, he swung them into the aisle. He was studying her again, and Angel squirmed mentally.

"Is there such a thing as a crazy angel?" he said mockingly earnest. "It sounds funny — a contradiction."

That's exactly what I am, Jay — a contradiction, she thought, trying to stare him down. "I guess I can be sometimes," Angel said casually, finally giving up and looking away. "Isn't everyone crazy once in a while?"

"I'm not interested in *everyone*, Angel." He suddenly clapped a hand to his forehead. "Listen to me. I can't believe myself. I've never — I mean, *never* — said anything like that to a girl."

Angel had to laugh. "Maybe, but you'll get to say lots of things like that if you decide to be Danny Zuko."

"Ahhh, you've been talking to Jody, I see.

32

Did she tell you to brainwash me, Angel?"

"Yes," Angel admitted. "And I agree with her. If she says you can act, then you can. And Danny is supposed to be good-looking, cool. . . ." It was her turn to clap a hand — over her mouth.

Oh, no. She had done exactly what she hated to have done to her. *I've been sitting here, thinking that we're really getting to know each other, and what I really was doing was admiring the way his hair curled, crisp and dark, and the cleft in his chin, and the way his mouth moves when he talks.*

Jay didn't look upset; just the opposite. He was smiling delightedly as if she'd just handed him a nice gift.

"Hey, thanks, Angel. Good-looking and cool. I never thought I'd ever hear *that.*"

She shrugged and tried to form a smile but she was wondering why he thought so little of himself. He *was* good-looking — and more important — very nice. Angel was surprised to realize that she liked him . . . quite a lot.

"Anyway, I've decided that I *will* audition tonight. Jody told me that you were going to be there, too. Don't laugh if I flub my lines, Angel."

She was honestly shocked. "I wouldn't do that, Jay."

He was already thinking about something else. "I like your bracelet. What's the little Pinocchio mean?"

She had to swallow hard before she could

say, "Oh . . . nothing much." *How come he had picked that charm to notice*? Her mouth was going dry again and her heart felt like it was beating too fast. *What did he know about her? Had Jody told him something? But what*? she wondered. *Jody doesn't know anything.*

"It's cute. I never saw one like that before. My mom has lots of charms on her bracelet. My father just bought her . . . a new one."

Angel wondered why his voice had been so hesitant, and why it had trailed off almost inaudibly. "I got all of these for my birthday last week," she answered. Wanting to change the subject, she said, "I'm glad you're going to try out for Danny. And I'm sure you'll get the part. Mr. Damian will be thrilled. He's the jittery type, and not having a Danny is making him a little crazy. It's going to be a fun show, don't you think?" She grinned before asking, "Hey, can you sing?"

"Sure I can," he laughed.

The strained look on his face had gone away, and he drummed on the table lightly. "I hear you're the brains behind all the drama club productions. Jody said nothing can work without you. You do the props, supervise the set construction, do most of the actual building, coach, design the program, sell tickets, and keep everything from falling apart. She says you handle all the details. Funny, I would have thought you'd want to be onstage, acting. You *look* like a star."

Angel ignored that. "Jody was building me up too much. I just help out. I'm definitely a backstage person."

They talked for a while longer, and then Angel told Jay that she had to get home. "Mom will be wondering where I am. I usually go straight home after school — you know, check in before I go anywhere. My mother worries a lot."

That was a lie. Angel hadn't meant to let it slip out. Mom worry? That was a laugh and a half.

"Hold on. I'm going your way."

Jay pulled out a crumpled dollar bill, smoothed it, then left it on the red formica table for a tip.

On the way home, Jay asked her about her hobby of building furniture.

"Did Jody tell you about that, too?" she asked.

"Yes. Jody and I talk all the time. We always have. I don't know what I would have done without her," he said seriously. "I consider her the best friend I have in the world."

Angel was silent. The pang she felt wasn't from jealousy, she was sure. It was just that he'd sounded so serious — *too* serious. She knew now that Jay was easily hurt . . . sensitive. And Jody had told her that he didn't trust many people. She wondered if she should discourage him, warn him away, because she couldn't even trust herself. She wanted so badly not to lie anymore, but she had already lied to Jay twice.

When he left her at the corner of her street and she watched him walk away and turn into Henderson Street, Angel knew that she wasn't going to discourage him. She was already looking forward to seeing him that night at rehearsal. He was going to make a great Danny.

Besides, Angel reasoned, the lies had been small ones. They weren't important. And she wasn't going to do it anymore.

Angel used the spatula to slide a second square of lasagna onto her plate. She helped herself to more salad, and another roll.

"Angel!"

She looked up quickly. "What? Did you say something?"

"Not really," Mom answered tartly. "I was just amazed at your appetite tonight. I'd advise you to go easy, Angel. That is, if you're going to look your best in the bathing suit competition." Angel saw her father wink at her mother.

"I guess we better fill her in, Ellen," Dad said, smiling at Angel. "Wait 'til you hear, Angel."

"Hear what?" Angel aready had a sinking feeling in her stomach. "What's this about a bathing suit competition?"

"We wanted to surprise you, honey," Mom said, putting down her fork. "Your father and I think you should enter the Miss American Teenager contest. We're sure that you could win the local one, Miss New Jersey

Teenager. Your father talked to Bill Blanchard yesterday, and he thinks you're just right for it. He's willing to put up company money to sponsor you. Aren't you thrilled? Don't you think —"

"Mom . . . Dad. . . . *No*! Absolutely not. I don't want to. I can't. I'd . . . I'd hate it."

She saw that her parents weren't smiling anymore.

"And what am I supposed to tell Bill Blanchard, Angel? It's all set."

Bill Blanchard was her father's boss. She knew he didn't want to look foolish, but he had no right to make plans for her like that.

"I'm sorry, I just can't," Angel said tonelessly. "I'm sorry if you're disappointed, but why should I have to parade around? I'd feel stupid. I'd *hate* every minute of it."

"*Why* should you parade around? Make an effort? For us, that's why. For yourself, too." Mom sighed. "You're beautiful, Angel, and we're proud of you. You could win easily."

Angel pushed her plate aside and stared at the blue tablecloth for a long moment. It was the same old story, she thought. *The only time they ever notice I'm around is when it has something to do with the way I look.* At that moment she hated them both.

"You're wrong about my winning easily," she said carefully, knowing that she was about to lie again. But this time she was glad. "I didn't tell you this, but about two weeks ago, we had a contest at school. The entire school, not just the junior class."

Mom sat up straighter. "And?"

"And I *didn't* win. Not even close. I guess you don't know, Mom, but there are lots of girls at Edgemont High better looking than me. Seventeen, to be exact. I came in eighteenth."

The look of shock on her parents' faces made her smile inwardly. *Good!* she thought. *Serves them right.*

"I just can't believe that, Angel. I'm sorry, but I can't."

"Check if you want to," Angel said airily. "It's true. Both Jody and Tania beat me. Jody was twelfth and Tania was seventh." This was too much for her parents to swallow, Angel thought nervously. She knew she had gone too far when her father's face turned red, and he set his coffee cup down hard.

"That's ridiculous! Your friends are very nice, but by no stretch of the imagination could I believe that anyone would think that they are prettier than you. Who ran this contest, I'd like to know?"

Her mother's expression was just as indignant. "I would, too. I have a good mind to call the school and find out about these *extracurricular activities.*"

Angel sighed. Her mother might just do it, she thought. If she called the school, no one would know what she was talking about. Mom would realize that her daughter had made it all up. She couldn't let that happen.

"I hope you don't call, Mom," Angel said

earnestly. "Please, don't. It would be so embarrassing. I'd die if someone found out you called."

"Oh, well, then I won't, I guess. If it would make you feel bad. But, darling, not winning a silly school contest shouldn't discourage you. A state contest is much more sophisticated and we really do think you have an excellent chance. I hope you'll change your mind."

She knew she had to wipe the newly hopeful expressions from their faces. It didn't bother her at all, because she was really angry now. They just wouldn't quit.

"No, Mom. I can't. I won't. Please don't ask me again."

Her parents exchanged looks. "Well, if that's how you really feel, Angel," her mother said, "then it's settled."

"I'm glad you understand. I have to hurry now or I'll be late for rehearsal. I told you that we're putting on *Grease*, didn't I?"

"What part are you playing?" asked her mother, giving her a sharp look.

"I'm the stage manager, Mom. Just like last year."

"I don't understand you, Angel," her mother said sadly. "Why do you always choose to be backstage? Wouldn't you like to shine for a change?"

"I'm happy backstage," Angel said quietly, pushing her chair back and standing up. "I've got to get ready. Tania's dad is picking me up in ten minutes."

Her mother stared at her critically. "You are going to brush your hair and put on some blush, aren't you? You look washed out, Angel."

I am, Angel wanted to say. *You and Dad just put me through the wringer.* She left the room without another word.

Four

Angel stood by the bay window in the living room and waited. When she saw Tania's father's pickup truck turning into her street, she left the house, running along the curving path to the sidewalk. When Mr. James pulled over to the curb, she smiled and stuck out her thumb, hitchhiker-style.

"Going my way?" she asked.

"Did you notice what was in the back, Angel?" Tania asked when Angel got settled on the seat beside her. "Tell her, Dad."

"Well, Angel, I did it. Came across a '57 Chevy convertible. Red. It's disassembled, but it will be easy enough for your crew to put it together onstage. I brought along the bolts, and a small can of paint so you can touch up the rust spots. It's an old baby, not in the greatest condition, but —"

"Oh, Mr. James, I love you," Angel said, and meant it. Tania's dad always came through for her. Quite a few times he had come up with the hardest-to-find props in the nick of time. This time he was early.

Unlike her own father, Harold James was keenly interested in anything Tania was involved in. When Angel and Tania decided to go out for track, Mr. James was on the field with his stopwatch every Saturday and Sunday. He was always willing to drive them to the movies or the roller-skating rink, and a few times he'd put on skates and taught them some fancy moves. Many times Angel had envied Tania. She wondered if her friend knew how lucky she was. Mrs. James was great, too. She always made Angel feel welcome at their house.

By the time Mr. James stopped at Jody's house, Angel was relaxed and laughing. Tania was teasing her father about putting on weight.

"Angel, is she saying I'm fat? My own daughter? Now I ask you. . . ."

She had to laugh. Tania and her father did this kind of thing all the time, and when she was with them, she was expected to join in. It was usually fun. "Don't ask me, Mr. James. Please. I'll be in trouble, too."

He took one hand off the wheel, and patted his stomach. There was no doubt that he had gotten quite a bit bigger.

"Hah! I don't know what's the matter with you girls. Can't you lie? A little white lie never hurt anyone. For instance, you could say: 'Oh, Mr. James, how sleek and well-fed you are.' You try it, Angel. Lie a little."

It was all in fun, but Angel's smile was a little weak.

"Oh, Mr. James, how sleek and well-fed you are."

He insisted that Tania repeat it. They all laughed again as Jody came toward the car. He'd only been kidding, but his reference to little white lies made her nervous. She could have told him that he was dead wrong — that even a small lie could hurt someone. She knew about that.

Angel saw Jay jogging toward them. Jody motioned for Angel to roll the window down. "Hope you don't mind, Mr. James," Jody said breathlessly. "You have another passenger. Meet Jay Butler. He's going to be my leading man."

"Maybe," said Jay. "I'm just auditioning tonight."

Jay offered polite hellos to Mr. James, Tania, and Angel. "Jody and I can ride in the back, okay with you?"

"Okay with me if you don't mind sharing space with a Chevy. Take a look at it, Jay. It's a gem," said Mr. James.

It was a short ride to Edgemont High, but when they arrived Angel's spirits had lifted and a warm feeling had replaced the bitter one. She just wasn't going to think about her parents for the next few hours. Her life wasn't totally tough; she had good friends. Even Jay seemed happier now. He had needed friends, too.

"I just had the greatest idea, you guys," Tania said, when they had hopped down from the cab of the truck. "Look at that moon up there. It has inspired me. October. A full moon. Night. Cool weather. Now what does all that make you think of?"

"I'll bite." Jody, said.

"Halloween?" Angel guessed.

"Not quite," Tania said smugly. "A hayride. A big harvest moon, a pile of hay, and someone with a guitar or a portable radio. Doughnuts and cider afterward. Pops, you had hayrides when you were young; Mom told me all about them. Sounds like so much fun. And we could use this truck, couldn't we?"

"Hold your horses *and* the hayride, Tania," her father said pleasantly. "How many kids do you think would fit in this dinky pickup? You'd need a regular haywagon and a team of horses. It has to be done right, or not at all. Tell you what, honey, let me look into it."

Tania threw her arms around her father and hugged him tight.

"Pops, I love you."

A few minutes later, Tania whispered to Angel and Jody, "I can invite Bobby. He'll *have* to come to Edgemont for this."

Angel nodded, and thought that Jay would probably ask her to be his date. That was a nice feeling. *Only yesterday*, Angel thought, *I wouldn't have known who to ask*. She knew Jody wouldn't have any trouble finding a

44

date. Lots of boys liked Jody Farringer, even if only as a friend.

Jay helped Mr. James carry in the heaviest portion of the car. Jody and Angel teamed up to carry a pair of doors, and Tania rolled two heavy tires toward the side door nearest the auditorium. The tires kept getting away from her, and she was hysterical with laughter.

It took one more trip for the group to get the rest of the car into the school. Jay hadn't said a word to her besides hello. He was terribly nervous, Jody had told her quietly. Angel thought Jay did look terrified. She hoped that Mr. Damian would go easy on him.

He did. After only a few minutes into the first scene, Mr. Damian clapped his hands, and announced, "Our problems are over, group. We have our Danny. Welcome aboard, Jay."

Angel understood why Mr. Damian was so pleased. Jay's reading had been excellent. The director was a very small man, slim but muscular, with a lot of gray and black frizzy hair. He was always moving, his hands were never still, and sometimes, Angel thought, he seemed more like a conductor of a symphony orchestra than a director of a high school production. She liked him a lot, but he could be sarcastic and difficult at times. Mr. D, as the students usually called him, could really put together a play, though. He worried, he had fits, and he pulled at his hair fiercely when things went wrong. For the moment — because the part of Danny had finally been filled — he was calm. In his standard outfit — a black turtleneck and trousers — she decided he looked like a happy elf.

Mr. Damian wanted Angel to stand by and prompt for a quick but complete run-through of the script. "Butler will probably need lots of help," the director told Angel. "Jody said he's new at this."

Suddenly, Mr. Damian was muttering and yanking at his salt-and-pepper frizz. "An understudy. Angel, we have to have an understudy for Danny. But who? No one even comes close to looking like Danny Zuko, except Butler." He raised his voice, then ran to the very edge of the bare stage. "Is anyone out there? Help!"

Angel didn't dare look at Tania or Jody. She knew that Mr. Damian would come down hard if he thought they were laughing at him. This was a very serious problem, and until he solved it, Angel knew he would be impossible.

None of the boys looked anything like John Travolta. Of course, makeup, a black leather jacket, white t-shirt, black pants, boots, and a fifties hairstyle would make all the difference. Angel looked over at Jay and tried to imagine him with his hair slicked back and pomped in front, and with sideburns. He'd look really good, she decided.

"Can't anyone help me? Hey, you fellas in the wings. Step out onstage for a second.

Right now." Mr. Damian was hopping from one foot to the other. "Move!"

Reluctantly, five boys walked out on the stage in a ragged line. Some of them looked scared witless.

"Okay, one by one, turn slowly. Good heavens, doesn't anyone know what 'turn' means?"

The director was getting hysterical, but no one except the boys in the lineup seemed bothered. Angel wasn't. She had seen him in action often enough to know that he would immediately change into a pussycat if he found what he was looking for.

"You there, in the brown sweater. Turn and face me."

Angel saw that it was Steve Ellis. She was pretty sure that Mr. Damian would lose interest when he looked him over. For one thing, he wasn't tall enough, and not even a heavy leather jacket would hide the bony shoulders, prominent adam's apple, and slightly sunken chest. Not only that, but Steve had blond hair and pale brown freckles all over his face. It wasn't that Steve was a terrible or inexperienced actor. In fact, a few times Angel had seen him turn a small, insignificant role into something really special with the audience cheering him on. "Oh, Steve." Mr. Damian had been so excited that he hadn't even recognized him. Steve had been a member of drama club for a year longer than Angel and Jody had. Tania had just joined this year.

"Sure, you'll be okay," Mr. Damian was saying to Steve. "Wouldn't bother you if you had to wear a wig, would it, Ellis? Fine, pay attention then. Angel will find you a script. Okay, okay — let's go. Take your places everyone. Act one, scene one."

The crisis was over, and Angel ran to the open area at the back of the stage and opened the drawer of the old teacher's desk that served as her headquarters. Luckily, she had thought to make extra copies of the script.

She hurried back and handed the stapled manuscript to Steve. "Good luck," she whispered.

"Tell me how I get into these things," he whispered back and groaned. "This time I only wanted to pound nails and use a paintbrush."

Steve was a really nice kid, she thought as she walked away. But if Jay was shy and a little too sensitive, Steve was much more so. Except for drama club, he wasn't involved in school activities, and he didn't seem to have any friends. When he wasn't acting or helping with sets or props, he usually had his nose in a book. He seemed comfortable with very few people, and Angel was flattered that he even talked to her. No question about it, Steve was not the type to play a cool, macho character like Danny Zuko.

He probably won't ever have to. The thought made Angel feel better. Poor Steve. He really had looked awfully desperate.

"No, no, Ellis. Get out of the way. Watch

and listen from the wings, please."

Angel saw the blush infiltrating the freckles, and she felt sorry for him and angry at the director. Why did he always have to be so cutting? Anyone could see that Steve wasn't the type to laugh off harsh treatment.

Angel didn't have to prompt Jay once. He knew his lines perfectly. Most of the time he didn't even look at the script in his hands. Angel was impressed. She saw that Mr. Damian was, too. Not only had he memorized his lines, Jay had worked on moves, tone of voice, and had developed a swagger that was pure Danny. Even out of costume, he was wonderful, and at the end of act one, everyone in the auditorium, onstage and off, burst into applause. Angel watched as Jody stood on tiptoe and kissed Jay on the cheek. "I told you so," she said happily. "I just knew you'd be great."

Angel could see that Jay was embarrassed but also pleased by the attention. "You taught me every thing I know," he told Jody. Then he bent and kissed Jody lightly on the nose. "You're my good luck charm, Jody — never forget that," he said.

Angel had to turn away. She was ashamed of herself for feeling jealous because, after all, Jay and Jody were just good friends. Still, she couldn't help being disappointed that Jay hadn't come stand by her side when he heard the applause.

In fact, it wasn't until the end of rehearsal

that he seemed to realize that she existed. "I'm beat," he said, pretending to wipe sweat from his brow. "I used to think acting was a piece of cake. And, you, Angel, where have you been? Guess you had stuff to do in the back."

She didn't answer right away. The truth was, she had been so enthralled by his portrayal of Danny that she let her duties wait. Jody hadn't needed prompting either, but Angel chose to stand close by. And Jay hadn't even noticed she was there. "Mmmm, I was busy," she said. "I took care of a lot of little things."

"Jody says there's a soda machine in the teacher's lounge. Want a Coke? I sure do. My throat feels like someone dumped sawdust in it."

Angel followed Jay to the lounge. She was tempted to ask him why he didn't ask Jody instead, but she didn't.

"You're quiet tonight, Angel. Anything wrong?"

She shook her head, and she caught him looking at her hair. He grinned sheepishly. "Beautiful. Like corn silk, or something. I shouldn't tell you this, but you're beautiful even when you're not smiling."

She made a face and was about to protest out loud, but he didn't give her time. "Modest, too. I always thought beautiful girls were conceited. You're not, though. I like that."

He moved closer and for a split second,

Angel was sure that he was going to kiss her, but instead, he whispered. "Don't tell Jody this, but you look more like Sandy should. Jody's not the Olivia Newton-John type, but you definitely are." He smiled, then backed off a little. "Too bad you didn't try out. Don't you like acting?"

Angel shrugged, and tried to smile. "I'm not really good at it." She knew he'd intended the Olivia remark as a compliment for her and not as a criticism of Jody, but for an instant Angel wondered what would happen if she told Jody that Jay wanted her to be Sandy instead of her. Naturally, she wouldn't, but . . . what if?

"Want to ride home with Mr. James, or do you feel like walking?" Angel asked. "I need to walk. I'm so wound up."

"Sure. I could use a walk, too." It made her feel a lot better that Jay was choosing to be alone with her, instead of hurrying out to the pickup to talk to Jody.

"Are you hungry?" she asked. "If you are, when we get to my house, I can make cheeseburgers or something."

"Your parents won't mind? It's kind of late."

"No problem, Jay. Mom and Dad go to bed early on weeknights."

Angel found Tania and told her that they wouldn't need a ride home. Tania's dark eyes sparkled, "He must really like you, Angel."

Later at Angel's house, after they'd had cheeseburgers and Cokes, and there wasn't much more to talk about, Jay asked her if she'd be his date for the hayride.

"But we're not even sure there's going to be one," Angel said.

"*If* there is one. I just wanted to make sure no one else asked you first, Angel."

"The early bird gets the worm," Angel laughed.

Jay picked her hand up from the table and held it between his.

"That's the last thing I would call you. Worms aren't great looking, and you are, Angel Porter."

She sighed. She was going to have to ask him straight out if he liked her only for her looks. Not now, but soon. Maybe tomorrow she would find out.

$F^{\underline{ive}}$

A rehearsal was called for Wednesday night and Angel looked forward to it. She'd liked being part of all the productions, but it was even better now — Jay was part of it, too.

Angel liked him so much. The interest, the first faint attraction, had doubled. She caught herself doing strange things, being absent-minded, daydreaming. Every single time she picked up *Catcher in the Rye*, Angel had to spend a few minutes trying to remember where she had left off.

She was cagey with Jody and Tania. When they quizzed her about her feelings for Jay, she just shrugged. Since Monday night she had spent a lot of time with him. Jay waited for her after many of her classes, held her hand as they walked through the hall, and sat beside her at lunchtime. On Tuesday, he waited for her after school and asked her if she wanted to go to Archer's Deli again. She wasn't very hungry, but he was. While Angel watched, he demolished a double cheeseburger and three slices of pizza.

She entertained him with tales of past drama club productions. She exaggerated a lot but at least she didn't lie outright. The truth — embroidered a bit around the edges — made him laugh out loud.

"You're a good storyteller, do you know that?" Jay asked.

Angel managed not to laugh, when she said, "I've had a lot of practice." She left it at that.

On Wednesday after school Angel was sitting on the front steps watching for Jay to come through the doors. Jody appeared instead with a message from him. "He said to tell you that he had stuff to do at home, and that he would talk to you later. He'll be at rehearsal tonight," Jody said, then added, "At least, I hope he will be."

"Why do you say that, Jody?" Angel asked, frowning. "What's to prevent him from coming?"

"Oh . . . nothing, really," Jody said vaguely. "Come on, let's you and me go to Archer's. I could use a Coke and some advice on wardrobe for the play. Mr. Damian said you've already made notes about costumes and props."

Jay didn't show up for rehearsal. Angel couldn't understand it. Mr. Damian was steaming mad and he took it out on everyone. But he came down especially hard on Jody.

"Our male star has better things to do this evening," he announced sarcastically. "He had the decency to phone, but with a weak excuse. Our Danny chose to *babysit* this evening."

"Our leading lady recommended him so highly, and I must admit that I was pleased with his initial reading. However, I cannot afford to cast unreliable people in this play. It is not fair to me or to you."

Mr. Damian's features twisted into a sneer. "I'm afraid to ask — is the understudy here tonight? Or did he perhaps decide to take in a movie?"

"I'm here, Mr. Damian." Angel sighed with relief when Steve Ellis stepped from the shadows and crossed stage left to the director.

Steve stood, round-shouldered, and seemed helpless as Mr. Damian looked him over from head to toe. When Angel saw the director wince insultingly, she had the urge to toss her clipboard at him. "I do hope you've *glanced* at the script, Ellis. It would help."

"Yes sir," Steve said, and his adam's apple bobbed alarmingly. "I'll do my best, sir."

"You're going to need more than a wig," Mr. Damian added, and again, Angel felt the heat rise in her cheeks. The man was terrible, a tyrant, and he had no right to abuse Steve or make cutting remarks about Jay. She considered telling the director exactly what she thought of him. He'd never been easy to work with, but he was getting much worse, Angel decided.

Mr. Damian beat her to it. He walked across the stage and when he got close, he whispered to Angel. "Do me a favor, Angel. Next time I act like a monster, stick out your tongue at me, boo, scream, anything. Ellis didn't deserve that just now. He's a fine actor, and a nice kid. I just get carried away sometimes. My wife constantly tells me about it."

Her anger faded. "Next time I'll get everyone to boo and hiss, I promise."

"Thanks, Angel," he said and smiled before continuing. "Steven doesn't quite bring the magic to the role that your friend Butler did, but Ellis has something special, too. Ever notice how he steps out of his own personality and into a role as if he's stepping into a new set of clothing? He's an actor to the bone, Angel. I should tell him that some time; he needs his ego boosted. Instead, I knock it down every chance I get. I guess I really am a monster."

Angel noticed that the director minded his manners throughout the entire first act. He was gentle and extremely polite. Jody and Tania both kept glancing over at Angel. She guessed that they thought she had something to do with the miraculous change in Mr. Damian.

Angel didn't even need to prompt Steve. He knew his lines and was confident enough to rehearse without a script. Mr. Damian was right about him, Angel thought. Steve made everything look easy, and, amazingly, he almost became the macho leader of the Thunderbirds. Performing, even just during a read-through, made Steve come to life. He didn't seem shy, bewildered, or self-conscious. It didn't seem possible that he was the introverted loner she knew him to be.

At exactly nine o'clock, Mr. Damian called a break and everyone scattered. Angel, Tania, and Jody headed for the door that led to the lounge.

"Let's go outside for a few minutes," Tania suggested. "We can check out the moon and dream about the hayride."

It had been another warm, sunny day, and the night air was cool and fragrant with the scent of drying leaves and grass. Angel took a deep breath and tilted her head back and stared at the moon.

"Isn't it beautiful?" Angel held up her hands. "A real harvest moon. I love it. A hayride is a great idea, Tania. I'm glad you thought of it."

"*I'm* just terrific," Tania said, "although my mother gave me the idea. She and her friends did a lot of fun things when they were our age. Hayrides, picnics, progressive dinners. What do we do? Angel builds furniture on the weekends, Jody hangs out in the mountains, and I travel miles to see Bobby."

Angel was only half listening. "Jody? Did Jay really have to babysit? I mean, it doesn't make sense. Just yesterday he was so gung-ho."

"It couldn't be helped. Missing rehearsal wasn't Jay's idea."

Angel let the subject drop, but she wondered why Jody sounded so defensive. Could she be mad at Jay for letting her down? Something had happened, but Jody didn't look like she wanted to talk about it. *Which isn't really fair,* Angel thought. *Jody knows very well that Jay likes me. Why is she acting as if he wouldn't want me to know?*

"Steve was really good, wasn't he?" Tania said. "He learned the part in two days. He didn't even have to look at the script — not once."

Jody bumped Tania with her hip. "Is that a dig for me, friend?"

"Noooo . . ." Tania giggled. "But you *were* clutching your script for dear life."

Jody laughed, too. "I know my lines perfectly. Having the script in my hand just makes me feel more secure. You know that."

Jody took another sip from her can of Coke. "It doesn't surprise me about Steve. He takes everything he does very seriously. He didn't want to be understudy, but he didn't refuse. Steve would make a good Danny if anything happened . . . I mean, just in case." Jody looked a little nervous. "Steve is talented. Remember how good he was in *Arsenic and Old Lace?*"

"What do you mean — *just in case?*" Angel asked. "Do you know something I don't?"

Angel noticed that Jody avoided answering the question.

"All I'm saying is that Steve could do the

part if he had to. He's talented, and very professional."

"I don't understand you, Jody," Angel said, not able to hide her annoyance. She suddenly resented Jody's know-it-all attitude. "You're supposed to be Jay's best friend, aren't you?"

"Angel, I'm not saying I don't want Jay to be Danny."

"Well, that's what it sounds like. Besides, no matter what you two say about Steve's ability, Mr. Damian doesn't share your opinion."

"What do you mean?" Jody asked in a low voice. "What did our dear director have to say about Steve? Is that what he was whispering about before?

"Yes," Angel said irritably. "The only good thing he had to say about Steve was that he was reliable. He said . . ."

Angel felt strange, hot and prickly. She wanted to stop herself from saying these things, and as she reached for the charm that was supposed to help, she realized that she'd left the bracelet on the dresser in her room.

". . . some awful things. Not that I agreed with him."

"Come on, Angel — what?" Jody asked tensely.

She felt a wave of quiet sweep over her. "Mr. Damian said that Steve is too wimpy, too nondescript and low key to play Danny. He said Steve was a so-so actor, and hoped that Jay wasn't going to back out because otherwise *Grease* was going to be a big flop. He said that Steve couldn't hold a candle to Jay."

There was complete silence.

"Well, Jay *is* better. He was great," Angel said coldly. "We better get back now."

"Mr. Damian can go pound salt. What right does he have to say such terrible things. Besides, he's wrong," Jody said angrily.

"Mr. Damian is awful sometimes," Tania said. "Really mean. I'm not sure I like him at all."

How could she have told such a terrible lie?

"He said he was sorry later," she almost stammered. "He even called *himself* a monster."

"He *is* a monster," Jody said hotly. "I'm wondering if we should protest or something — if we have to, just drop out of the play. All of us. I think I'm going to tell him off."

"Oh, come on, Jody," Angel said, scared and nervous. Jody couldn't confront Mr. Damian. She just couldn't.

Angel, Jody, and Tania heard the noise at the same time. A rustling in the bushes, and then the sound of feet on the cement walk. It was dark, and they strained to see.

"Hey, what was that?" Tania asked breathlessly.

"Not what, Tania — *who*," Jody said grimly. "I hate to say this, but it was Steve Ellis. He probably heard every word we said."

"Oh, no . . . *no*," Angel moaned. "That's *terrible*."

It was. She hadn't meant for Steve to hear. She'd only wanted to show Jody that she was a better friend to Jay, more loyal, and that she . . . *Oh, no — what have I done?* Angel cried to herself.

"The poor guy. I feel so sorry for him," Tania said.

"I didn't know he was there," Angel said, aware of the whine in her voice. "I never would have said . . . repeated ,. . . those things."

Angel wanted to run after Steve, or do *something*. She felt like throwing herself on the ground, kicking and screaming because she knew it was too late. She had no way of backing out of it, though. No way at all.

"I suppose we have to go in and do act two. I don't want to. Do you, Jody?"

"Uh uh," Jody told Tania. "Mr. Damian's going to wonder why Steve took off, and I'm going to tell him. It's his fault."

"You can't tell him, Jody," Angel said desperately. "Mr. Damian confided in me, and I shouldn't have told you and Tania. He never meant for Steve to hear it. You'll get me in big trouble. *You can't say anything.*"

"I don't know, Angel," Jody said doubtfully. "He shouldn't get away with it."

"Please." Angel said. "Don't do this to me."

Reluctantly, her friends agreed to keep quiet, and also pretend that they had no idea why Steve hadn't returned after break.

Angel was so relieved that she almost burst into tears. The rest of the rehearsal passed in a haze of confusion that Angel knew was mostly in her own mind. She kept dropping things, and her typewritten lists blurred before her eyes. She just wanted to go home, crawl into bed, and pull the covers over her head.

Jody and Tania didn't seem to have anything to say on the way home, and Angel was glad. What could she say?

Even after she huddled in bed and closed her eyes, she couldn't go to sleep. With her eyes wide open, Angel stared into the inky blackness. All the lies she'd ever told — the small ones as well as the ugly ones — paraded before her in rapid succession, like grubby sheep jumping a broken-down fence.

The lie about Steve Ellis was the grubbiest of all. Angel felt dirty, and her sleep was troubled when it finally came.

When light crept into her bedroom, Angel realized that she was going to have to face the day. Then tears finally came, the wetness soothing her tired, dry eyes.

When she got out of bed and saw herself in the big mirror over the dresser, she quickly turned away. Face the day? How could she if she couldn't even stand to face herself? The tears came faster, and it was a long time before she had the heart to get ready for school.

S^{ix}

The only way Angel could make it through the school day was to make a solemn vow that she would never, ever — no matter what — tell another lie. She was going to stop. *No,* she amended, *I have already stopped.* Last night's lie was the last one, and, she knew, the worst one.

It was going to be hard to pretend that she was fine today, and that she hadn't just spent the most miserable night of her life.

Angel wondered if the cold wet towels she'd held against her eyes for five minutes had really done the trick and taken away the red puffiness. She didn't have time to check again, not if she wanted to be on time to meet Tania, Jody, and Jay, and walk to school with them.

Angel had to pretend that she was fine. Pretending wasn't the same as lying, she thought. Acting was pretending, and there was nothing terrible about that. Theater was what all her friends were so hooked on, she decided, and if she had to play the role of an innocent cheerful angel, she would.

It would be dangerous if she moped or made too much of what had happened the night before. If Jody and Tania thought that Angel was suffering because of Mr. Damian, they would go after him and confront him with what Angel had repeated.

Repeated? It made her sick, thinking of the way the words had tumbled out so easily. Slick, slippery, evil words, she thought, remembering that was the way her lies usually happened. No click of warning, no good reason, but easy, so ridiculously easy. She always hated herself afterward.

It was another nice day, too warm for a jacket. She was glad she hadn't packed away her summer clothes. She slipped a red pullover over her head. She couldn't remember when she'd ironed the white oxford-cloth shirt, but it was crisp and clean against the red wool sweater. Angel sighed, feeling like an imposter. Crisp and clean? Not the right description for the way she felt inside.

She left the house and hurried to the corner. Looking to the left she saw that her friends were far down the street. Not that she could blame them. Glancing at her watch, Angel saw that she was almost ten minutes late. "Hey, you guys — wait for me."

Jay seemed fine, and very glad to see her. He caught her hand in his, and pulled her along. "About time," he said teasingly. "I didn't think you were coming. Tell her, Jody, how disappointed I was."

Angel's immediate thought was, *Why do I need her to tell me?*

"His heart was broken. Tania and I vouch for that," Jody said, laughing. "I wasn't sure he'd make it through the day."

And you know him so well, right? Angel couldn't seem to control the nasty thoughts. But why, she wondered, did Jody always have to let everyone know that she could speak for Jay, that she knew him better than anyone, including Angel.

"My heart was broken last night," Angel said. "I missed you. I couldn't believe it when I heard it when you were babysitting."

Jody and Jay exchanged glances that Angel was sure they hadn't meant for her to see. What was going on? What did Jody know? It was obvious she shared some kind of secret with Jay.

"Something came up at the last minute, that's all." His tone was so final, almost cold. Angel decided not to question him anymore, at least not in front of Jody and Tania.

Instead, Angel acted extra cheerful. "Isn't this the most gorgeous day? I feel so great. It's partly the weather and partly that I've decided not to worry about a thing. How's Pops doing, Tania? Did he find a haywagon yet?"

For the rest of the way to school, the conversation was light and easy, and — most important — safe. Angel was grateful that Tania and Jody didn't mention anything about Steve or Mr. Damian. She figured that

Jody didn't want to worry Jay, or make him feel guilty for not making it to rehearsal. Angel hoped that Jody wouldn't mention it to him ever.

Relief made her talkative, and Angel found herself telling them about how her parents had wanted her to enter the Miss New Jersey Teenager contest. She'd meant to make them laugh, but Jay didn't seem to think the idea was a bad one. "Why don't you? I wouldn't mind saying that my girl is —"

Jody and Tania had pounced on him, pounding him on the back and messing up his hair. "Gotcha!" Jody said. "Don't tell us it was a slip of the tongue either. Tell me, Angel, since when have you been Jay Butler's girl?"

They were teasing, and ordinarily Angel would have laughed along with them, but she wished that they would mind their own business. She forced a smile, though. Maybe it was lack of sleep that was making her feel so unsociable.

Jay squeezed her hand. "Don't mind them."

Shrugging, Angel looked ahead, and saw that the school steps were deserted. "Hey, we're late. Let's hurry."

A minute later Angel knew what it meant to be saved by the bell.

At lunchtime Angel was so tired she couldn't eat. Jody leaned close and asked her what was the matter.

66

"Oh, nothing. I didn't sleep too much last night."

Jody nodded. "I know you felt bad, Angel. About Steve, I mean. You shouldn't blame yourself, though. It wasn't you who said those terrible things about him. I still think we should confront Mr. Damian."

"No!"

Everyone sitting at the long lunch table turned to look at her. Angel ducked her head.

Luckily, Jay had gone back to the lunch counter for another dish of Jell-O. She saw him heading back toward their table and then, when he was just a few feet away, heard Don Kiernan calling to him. Angel wasn't the only one who heard, "Hey Butler. You better get to the next rehearsal. Mr. Damian's calling you unreliable. I'd straighten him out if I were you."

Jay said something to Don that Angel couldn't hear and then came over to the table and sat down beside her. He put the Jell-O down on the table and exploded.

"Unreliable? Where does he get off? I take the time to call him and explain, and he goes talking behind my back? I have a good mind to show him just how unreliable I can be."

Angel could feel the heat of his anger, and she leaned as far away from him as she could, suddenly frightened. She prayed that he would get off the subject of Mr. Damian.

"I'm supposed to skip off to rehearsal and leave my little brother and sister alone in the house while Mom is . . ."

He slumped and stopped talking abruptly. Jody clamped her lips together, but was staring at Jay with concern in her dark eyes. After a few seconds, she looked down at the table and said very softly, "Don't worry about it, Jay. Don't worry at all. Mr. Damian is just a jerk sometimes."

Angel sucked in her breath, and closed her eyes. She wasn't ready for what was coming. Tears stung the insides of her eyelids. If Jay found out what the director had said — or what Jody thought he had said — about Steve, he would be so furious, he might . . .

"Yeah, I've heard. Don't worry, I'm not going to quit. I told you, Jody, I really want to be in this play."

Angel excused herself and forced herself to walk — not run — to the girls' room. She knew Jay and her friends expected her to come back to the cafeteria, but she couldn't. Until the bell rang, she would stay in the quiet, tiled room and rest.

When Angel found that Jay wasn't waiting for her after class that day, she didn't even mind. She really didn't want to talk to anyone. She needed sleep, and nothing else. She had almost reached Room 101 for sixth period math when she saw them. Jay and Jody were standing together, and it appeared that Jay was doing some serious talking. Jody was listening intently, looking up into his face. Angel felt a sharp twinge, like someone had just stuck her with a dozen pins. Who was Jody kidding? Angel wondered. It was obvious that she liked Jay a lot. And it was just as obvious that Jay chose to tell Jody things that he didn't tell her. Important things. *He saves the fluff for me*, Angel thought bitterly.

After school, Angel didn't bother to stop at her locker. She had slipped three heavy books into a crowded bookshelf in her homeroom to save time. She hurried through a side door and cut across the parking lot, heading toward home. She didn't stop until she was safely inside her house.

Angel heard her mother typing in the small den opposite the downstairs powder room. She debated whether or not she should disturb her to tell her that she was home.

Why should I? Angel wondered. *If she wants me, she can look for me.*

Angel didn't bother getting undressed. She fell across her bed and before her thoughts focused again, she was asleep. She woke up two hours later to the sound of a voice calling her name. Angel wasn't sure whether the voice was part of her dream, and it took her several seconds to struggle into a sitting position.

"Pick up the phone, Angel. You're keeping him waiting."

Stumbling to the phone in her parents' bedroom, Angel was thinking that this was the first time Jay had called her.

It wasn't Jay, it was Mr. Damian. Angel's mouth went dry when she heard his voice. She knew he had found out. That was why

Jody and Jay were talking in the hall between classes. They had been planning their attack on the director.

"I never thought you were the nap type, Angel. Do me a favor, will you? I won't be in school tomorrow. Type up a notice and stick it on the bulletin board. I'm calling a rehearsal for tomorrow night. I forgot to mention it Wednesday."

"Sure."

"What? I can't hear you, Angel."

"I said, sure, Mr. Damian. I'll do it right now."

He laughed. "Right now, go back to sleep. Just take care of it first thing in the morning, all right?"

"All right. Yes. Sure, Mr. Damian."

Angel replaced the receiver in its cradle and sank down on the thick gray carpeting and leaned back against her parents' bed. She stared up at the silvery-white ceiling for a long time.

She heard her father's voice this time, calling her down to dinner. She got up slowly and dragged herself downstairs to the dining room.

"Angel! You look terrible," Mom explained, her eyes wide with distaste. "You have big circles of makeup under your eyes, and your hair is all over your face."

"Do I look like a raccoon?" Angel asked dully.

"Like something the cat dragged in," her father said, smiling.

"I really do?" Angel said, pulling out her chair, and gazing without interest at the rich, rare roast surrounded by heaps of steaming wild rice.

"You could have washed your face and done something with your hair before you came downstairs," Mom said irritably. "I would think you'd hate to look like such a mess. Most girls would give their right arm to have your looks."

Angel looked up and stared at her parents with horrified wonder. "You really think so, don't you? You really think I should care that much!"

Her parents looked surprised. "Of course, you should, Angel. You've been especially blessed."

It wasn't going to change. She repeated just what she'd said to Mr. Damian over the phone. "All right. Yes. Sure, Mom."

As if she were sleepwalking, Angel got up from her chair and left the dining room. She went upstairs to the bathroom and used vaseline to remove the smudged eye makeup and scrubbed her face until it glowed pink. She brushed her teeth. She spent several minutes brushing her hair until it fell into its usual smooth pattern. She put on lipstick. Then, with her head held high, she went back downstairs and into the dining room. She stood in the archway until her parents looked up.

"How do you like me now, Mom? Dad? Are you happy?"

They still didn't get it.

"We love you, Angel. And we're very happy with you. You know that. Someday you'll be glad that we kept after you to look your best." Mom beamed at her and Dad followed her example.

The roast beef could have been cardboard. The rice kept sticking in her throat. She washed it down with two glasses of milk and didn't wait for dessert.

"I have scads of homework. I'd better get to it."

It was a lie, but Angel didn't worry about it. She couldn't stand to sit with her parents for another moment. She had just pushed back her chair when the phone rang.

"I'll get it," Angel said, rushing into the hall. It was the second time in one day that a bell had saved her.

This time it *was* Jay.

"Just thought I'd call and find out what happened to you this afternoon. I looked for you. Jody said she thought you weren't feeling well, and went right home."

And Jody knows everything, doesn't she? "She was right. I came home and slept for a couple of hours. I've just finished dinner. What are you doing?"

He hesitated. "Ahhh, not much. Keeping an eye on the kids, that's about all. I have to read a couple of chapters after they go to bed. Our English teacher assigned *Catcher in the Rye*, too."

"How about that? Are you babysitting again?"

There was another long pause. "Jay? Are you there?"

"Mmmm, yeah. Sort of babysitting. Mom doesn't . . . ah, she doesn't feel good. She's sleeping."

"What a good boy," Angel said lightly. Jay never said anything about his family, but it really seemed that his parents depended on him a lot.

"Not really," Jay said. "Would you hold on a minute? Michelle can't reach the water faucet and she's pestering me for a drink."

"I'll hold on."

It took him quite a long time to return to the phone, and Angel could hear children's voices and Jay's deeper one.

"I'm trying to imagine you as a big brother," Angel told him when he returned. "Instead, Danny Zuko is the image I keep getting."

Angel told him that Mr. Damian had called. "Rehearsal tomorrow night. Are you going to make it?"

"Sure," Jay said gruffly. "Why wouldn't I?"

Angel thought he sounded mad.

"I don't know. Maybe you'll have to baby-sit again." Angel was afraid she had sounded sarcastic, so she hurried to cover it. "What I mean is that if your mother's still sick she might need you, and —"

"I'll be there," he said in that strange, gruff voice. "Don't worry about it. Listen I'll see you tomorrow, okay. The kids are yelling for me."

"Okay. Bye, Jay."

Angel wished she hadn't been so pushy about the rehearsal, but why did everyone else in his life seem more important to him than her? Why had he bothered to call anyway? The more Angel thought about it, the madder she got. She could bet that if it were Jody he called, Jay wouldn't have made such a weak excuse to get off the phone.

She sat up straight suddenly and stared at the phone. Jay hadn't sounded too happy at the end of their conversation; was it possible that he had called Jody immediately afterward to cry on her shoulder? He wouldn't do that, would he? Had *he* lied to her? She hadn't heard the kids yelling at him.

Angel reached for the phone and then quickly punched in Jody's number. If she answered, Angel decided, she could just say she was calling to tell her about tomorrow night's rehearsal.

Jody's line was busy.

Taking a deep breath, Angel broke the connection, and punched 411 for information. In two minutes she had Jay's number, and without hesitating, punched it in.

His line was busy, too.

Angel stood up after she replaced the receiver and climbed the stairs to her room. She shut her door and leaned against it. She felt numb.

Slowly, she slid down until she was sitting on the floor, and after a minute, she put her face in her hands.

At this very moment — as the tears leaked out and slowly made their way down her face — Jody and Jay were probably deep into a satisfying conversation.

Maybe they were talking about her. Jay could be telling Jody that he had decided that looks weren't everything, and that he wanted her to be his girl instead of Angel. It was possible, she decided.

$S\underline{even}$

Angel swam to the surface of heavy, rolling sleep as the voice somewhere above her repeated her name over and over again. "Angel. Angel." There was a chorus, much louder. "Get up. Get up. You have to get up now."

With great effort she opened her eyes. Her mother was standing at the foot of her new bed. "Mom. What is it? What's up?"

The annoyed expression relaxed into a smile. "You, I hope. Angel, it's a good thing I checked. You forgot to set your alarm. Did you also forgot that this is the day your father and I will be spending the afternoon and evening in the city?"

Angel blocked a yawn with her fist. "How could I forgot something I never knew?"

The frown reappeared and her mother fidgeted with the rope of pearls around her neck. "Oh, Angel, of course we told you." She looked away and added vaguely. "I'm sure of it."

"Why so early?" Angel said, sitting up.

"There's a company breakfast, followed by a sales conference. The annual awards luncheon is in the afternoon. Your father also managed to pick up tickets for a show," she smiled. *"Sugar Babies . . .* how about that?"

"Sounds great. Mom, is it really only six o'clock?" Angel groaned and flopped back on her pillows.

Her mother was halfway through the door. "Don't go back to sleep, Angel," she warned. "You don't want to be late for school."

I don't? Angel mused. Actually, it was an excellent idea. She should be feeling very well rested after a nap in the afternoon and a long night's sleep. Instead she ached all over and her throat felt kind of scratchy. Angel thought she might really be coming down with something. "Mom? Are you still here?"

Angel waited for her mother to call out, "What, Angel?" but there was silence. A few seconds later, she heard the muffled roar of the Buick as it backed out of the driveway. Angel didn't bother looking out the window. They were gone. If she wanted to stay home she could.

Angel lay back on her bed and looked around her room. In the stark morning light, her room looked like a studio, she thought. She gazed with pleasure at one of the new shelves opposite her bed with the row of books and bristly little cactus plants. Every week since school started she had bought a new plant, and now there were many different types of cacti in dark green plastic pots.

She liked the bamboo blinds rolled up halfway to let the light in, and grimaced when she thought how hard Dad had tried to convince her to put up conventional curtains, preferably in ruffled pastel. Mom had been horrified when Angel brought home the brown-and-white batik print contour sheet and announced that it was her new bedcover.

When summer ended, Angel begged for the best of the patio plants, and the dracaena palm and the Boston fern were thriving in her airy, sun-drenched room.

"Must you make it so masculine, Angel? It's so strange and spare and . . . well, jungle-ish."

What bothered her parents, she knew was her rejection of the expensive white French provincial bed and matching dressers, the ruffly, flower-print curtains and spread, the heavy, standing gilt-edged mirror, and the host of angels Mrs. Porter had collected since Angel's birth.

She hated those fat pink and white cherubs with puffy lips and prominent belly buttons. Gilt-framed prints of angels, plaster figurines, and miniature angels had cluttered the walls and every available surface. Angel had always felt as if she were sharing her bedroom with a hundred naked babies.

Her parents finally gave into her redecorating plans. They even paid for the wood and supplies, and a few necessary tools. The mattress for the platform bed hadn't been cheap. Angel teetered between gratitude and guilt for almost two weeks. They shouted at her, finally — a duet — and told her to please stop saying thank you.

They didn't understand what designing and building the furniture meant to her, or having a place of her own that really was her own — her ideas, her favorite colors and textures, her taste. Her room wasn't pretty at all, Angel thought. It was spacious, functional, restful, pleasing to her eyes.

She didn't have to hurry. She would go to school but later than usual so that she wouldn't have to face her friends right away. She needed time. She was afraid, simple as that. *What's going to happen?* she wondered over and over again, in the shower, blow-drying her hair, smoothing on makeup.

Angel was buttoning the cuffs of her navy blue shirt when the possibilities occurred to her — one by awful one. It was possible that Steve Ellis would stay away from rehearsal and Mr. Damian would phone to find out why, or Steve would show up angry and have it out with the director. It was also possible that Jody had already talked to Mr. Damian and already knew that Angel had made up the cruel things about Steve, and Jay already knew because Jody told him on the phone last night. Tania knew, too, everyone knew. When she arrived at rehearsal, the entire drama club would hiss and boo and throw rotten tomatoes at her.

Angel went downstairs and had a light breakfast. Wiping the crumbs from the table with a yellow sponge, Angel suddenly thought, *It's my word against Mr. Damian's.* Everyone knew how temperamental he could be, how sarcastic, and sometimes, obnoxious. It *was* his word against Angel's.

Now she couldn't wait to get out of the grating silence of her house and away from her terrible thoughts. She could never do it — blame Mr. Damian — no matter what happened. Besides, it was stupid to speculate about who would be on her side and who would be on his. Stupid and impossible, she thought, locking the door after her.

Angel had run out of the house too early. Jay and Jody and Tania were waiting for her, and from the looks on their faces, they were happy to see her. Nothing was wrong. Angel decided that she had made a huge ugly mountain out of a dinky little mole hill. As usual.

The day passed uneventfully. The forty-five minute study hall gave her time to think. Angel found herself working out an explanation for herself. What she worked out was more of an excuse, she thought. *I embroider the truth because I want people to like me. I'm a born storyteller, and a few times it has just gotten out of hand. I want to be interesting and I'm not sure of that unless I'm making them listen and. . . .*

Oh, it was so stupid, she thought irritably.

*After all, who really cares except me? I'm
not sure if I should care.*

The rest of the day was fine, lunchtime
especially. Jay was in a great mood, and very
attentive. Jody spent the lunch hour talking
to Don Kiernan. Later Jody confided to
Angel and Tania that she had asked him to
be her date for the hayride.

On the way home Angel debated whether
she should invite them over to her house. Her
parents weren't going to be home until late
evening, and she wasn't sure she could stand
being alone.

She decided not to. She didn't feel very
good at all. Her scratchy throat was sore
now, and her arms and legs were heavy and
achy. Maybe if she slept for a while she
would feel better. No matter what, she
couldn't miss rehearsal.

Two weeks ago she had rough-sketched
her ideas for the sets, but she definitely had
to get her crew working tonight. At least
the plywood was there, piled up backstage,
waiting to be pounded and painted into
shape.

The prop list was incomplete, and she
really had to check with the cast and see
what they could come up with in the way of
costumes. So much to do.

She fell asleep on the couch in the family
room in the middle of her favorite soap,
General Hospital. She was too tired to care
what Grant said to Celia, or what Jimmy Lee
said to Celia, or what Holly said to Celia.

Her skin felt hot but she dozed off while she was trying to remember where Mom kept the thermometer.

It was pitch dark when Angel woke up, and at first, she huddled deeper into the couch, fearful and feverish. She was sick ... so sick. She dragged herself off the couch and switched on the lamp on the end table. Peering at the mantle clock, she saw that it was twenty minutes of seven. Tania had said that her father was driving them again, and would be there at seven exactly.

Shakily, she walked to the kitchen and switched on the overhead light, and blinked hard, her eyes protesting the harsh glare. After a glass of orange juice and some cool water, her hands were still shaking so badly that she almost dropped the glass.

"I can't miss rehearsal," she moaned out loud. It took her fifteen minutes to pull herself together. Even then she knew she looked horrible, but her mother wasn't around to criticize and lecture her on the importance of looking her best.

It was only when she was squeezed into the back of Mr. James' Ford that Angel realized that she was exposing everyone to whatever she had. That's all Mr. Damian would need, she thought — the entire cast coming down with the flu.

It got worse as the minutes passed — her whole body burned and ached and begged to be put to bed. Jody and Tania were concerned when they reached the auditorium and saw her in the light from the white spotlight. "You should have stayed home, Angel," Jody said. "I can't believe your mother let you out of the house."

Angel admitted that her parents were away, and both of her friends scolded her for not calling them. "What are friends for?" Jody asked, putting a comforting arm around Angel's shoulders. "If you want, I'll call my mom. She'll take care of you until your mom and dad get home from New York."

It took some fast talking but Angel finally convinced them that she would be all right for a couple of hours. "I'll just do quiet things," she promised. "I'll work on my lists and sit through the whole rehearsal."

Jay hadn't noticed that she was sick, and Angel knew why. He was nervous again, and mixed with his jangled nerves, she could tell, was fury at the director. She could tell by the hard looks Jay kept sending in Mr. Damian's direction. Just so long as he sent looks and not words, Angel thought, shivering with apprehension.

She'd had the perfect excuse for not coming to rehearsal, but it had seemed important — in fact, urgent — that she be here.

In an instant Angel saw all her reasons trip and fall. It wasn't that she had so much to do — lists to go over, sets to build, and props to find. With absolute clarity she knew why she'd had to come, sick or not.

She needed to watch over things, make

sure that no one lost his temper and blurted out what had happened the night before during break. If she'd stayed away, she wouldn't have been able to control things. She had only a minute to bury her hot face in her hands before she was surrounded with eager workers with hammers in their hands.

"You don't need those yet," she said, trying desperately to smile. "Can any of you use a jigsaw?"

She found her sketches in the desk drawer and spread them out. Five boys almost bumped heads as they bent to study them.

"Suggestions and corrections are appreciated. These aren't to scale yet. I can do that tomorrow."

Don Kiernan glanced at her and shook his head. "The only thing you should do tomorrow, Angel, is visit a doctor. You're sick; why don't you go home?"

"Can't," she snapped. "Too much to do. Tell you what, Don. Drag some of that plywood over here and you can rough out some of these storefronts. And bring some two-by-fours."

"Attention, please. Listen up, everyone."

Mr. Damian stood stage center and held up his arms, and did a series of dance steps as he waited for the chatter to die down. If he was dancing, Angel decided, he couldn't be upset. So far, so good.

"First the good news," he announced dramatically. "The P.T.A. has done some of our work for us. They actually formed a committee to round up old fifties-style black leather jackets. It is my pleasure to tell you that everyone who needs one will have the real thing — we have all sizes."

There was a round of enthusiastic applause. Angel was thrilled. One less problem for her.

"And now, the bad news," Mr. Damian said, letting his arms fall to his sides. "We're losing precious time here. Our understudy for Danny has seen fit to drop out of the play. I understand from his messenger that Steve Ellis is quitting drama club altogether. I have to say that I don't have much admiration for quitters."

There was silence followed by excited buzzing. Everyone whispered at once. Angel caught phrases — "How come?" ". . . so loyal . . ." "What happened to . . ."

". . . the list, Angel," Mr. Damian said.

She reached up and ran a hand through her hair. It was damp with perspiration.

"Hey, Angel? Are you with us?"

Mr. Damian was walking toward her. "You look terrible. What kind of germs are you bringing to my rehearsal?"

He was joking, Angel thought, wasn't he? Why was he glaring at her?

"Anyway, please check the list and see if you can pick out one of the guys who didn't quite make it at auditions. We can stick him in as a gang member, and I'll put Don in as understudy. Kiernan? Put the hammer down and grab a script. And don't, I repeat *don't*, give me an argument."

"With this?" Don pointed to his carrot-colored curls, and mugged for the kids who stood in a semicircle behind Mr. Damian. "You can really see me as Danny Zuko?"

"Cut the comedy, Kiernan. What's the difference? Steve needed a wig, too."

"Mr. Damian?" Angel watched Jody walk across the stage to the director. Dread settled around her shoulders like a heavy jacket. Jody wasn't going to do it . . . was she?

"Yes, leading lady, what can I do for you?"

"I can help Don learn his lines. It would save time, and I'll bet Jay will give me a good recommendation as a coach."

"Fantastic!" Mr. Damian said, and a rare smile creased his small, foxlike face. "You're a doll, Jody, did anyone ever tell you that?"

"I'm just about to, Mr. Damian, sir." Don Kiernan walked over and put a friendly arm around Jody. "You're a doll, Jody, did anyone ever tell you that?"

The rehearsal went well after that. Angel couldn't wait to get home. In the car, Jay held her hand. Her parents weren't home when she got there, so Jody offered to stay over.

"You are a doll, Jody, but *no* thanks," Angel whispered weakly. "I'll be okay, don't worry. I just want to sleep."

Angel wished she could smile, but it was too much to ask after such a close call.

E^{ight}

Late Saturday morning Angel woke up and discovered that she wasn't sick anymore. A little weak and shaky, but the soreness in her throat, her fever, and the aches had all gone away. She also discovered that she was very hungry and remembered that she hadn't eaten dinner the night before.

She could tell that her parents felt bad about not being there for her. Dad whipped her up a cheese omelet while Mom made her a steaming cup of orange-spice tea. Angel felt pampered, and, for a change, well-loved, and soon she was a hundred percent well.

Mom and Dad wouldn't let her help clean up the kitchen and so she went back upstairs, took a shower, and washed her hair. By noon Angel was dressed and her hair was dry and shining. She didn't have any idea what she would do with the day. It was cold and gray, with a darker blanket of clouds just above the treetops. Maybe she should work on the wood cubes that were going to be her end tables. After she settled into it, the restlessness might go away.

She still hadn't made up her mind, when the phone rang. Eagerly, she ran across the hall to her parents' bedroom, yelling, "I've got it up here."

It was Jay, and Angel closed her eyes happily when she heard the tender concern in his voice. If he hadn't paid much attention to her last night, Angel felt that he was really making up for it now. "Are you sure you're okay, Angel?"

"Yes, really. Much better. It was just a twenty-four hour bug, I guess. I'm as good as new."

"Great. That's what I hoped to hear. Now you can go out with me tonight. I just found out that I can have the car, and, believe me, Angel, that doesn't happen very often."

"How's your mother feeling?"

"My mother?" There was a pause but Jay sounded quite cheery when he said, "She's much better, too. Doing real good. What about going out with me tonight? I have big plans if you say yes, Angel."

"Yes. So, what kind of plans?"

He laughed. "Well, I have some money that's burning a hole in my pocket. I figured I'd impress you — how does dinner and dancing sound?"

"Wow! Consider me impressed. That means I should dress up, right?"

"Right. You'll be a knockout whatever you wear, though. I might even break down and wear a sport jacket and tie. As soon as I get off the phone I'll make reservations. I haven't decided on a place yet, but I'll get right on it. I promised the kids — my brother and sister — that I'd take them to a Smurf movie this afternoon. Do you believe it?"

Angel laughed softly. "I *do* believe it. From what I know, I'd say you're a wonderful brother and son. You know, Jay, I always wished I'd had a brother — an older one, not a younger one."

"Mmmm, but don't expect me to act like your brother, Angel."

"I won't."

Angel put the phone back and returned to her room, smiling to herself. Jay had sounded so . . . so romantic when he'd said that. So sweet. Angel felt that the world had been out of kilter but now it was back in the right orbit. This would be her first real date, too. She wasn't going to count the junior high dances or those first, horribly awkward boy-girl parties.

Her parents were going to be thrilled. Angel knew they couldn't understand why she wasn't more popular. She guessed that they expected her to be beating boys off with a stick because of her looks. The truth was that she hadn't been terribly attracted to any of the boys she knew, and many of them seemed kind of intimidated by the fact that she was pretty.

Tania was exceptionally pretty, too, Angel thought, but because she was black, no one asked her out. Like Jody, she had scads of boy *friends*, but Tania had confided that her parents wouldn't approve of her dating anyone not of her own race. "Pops said there are too many heartaches involved in a mixed relationship. Mom says that things have changed, but not enough."

Jody just hadn't been interested enough. "When I'm rich and famous, that's when I'll look for love. I don't have time now."

Many of the girls in the junior class had been dating or going steady since sophomore year. Girls in the sophomore class were dating seniors. Angel smiled inwardly when she thought about telling Jody that she was a "late-bloomer." Late or not, Angel thought, dinner and dancing with Jay Butler had been worth waiting for. He had said that he would pick her up at six-thirty because that was as long as he could go without food.

What was she going to do all afternoon, Angel wondered, looking out of her window again. It wasn't such a great day; she'd been spoiled by the Indian summer.

The phone rang again and Angel raced for it. It was Jody, asking how she felt.

"Fantastic," Angel said so emphatically that Jody laughed.

"Sounds like a miracle. You felt so bad when I left you. Are you well enough to walk up to the mall with me? I have a list of things that I need, a few paperbacks, some notebook paper, a refill for my pen, and I thought I'd check out the winter jackets."

"Ready anytime you are. Shall we meet at the corner?"

"Great. Five minutes. See ya."

Angel put her arms around herself and hugged tight when she was back in her room and standing in front of the mirror. She smiled and said, under her breath, "Nothing to worry about. Nothing at all."

For the first time in a long time, Angel felt good inside, and it was true that everyone seemed to really care about her this morning.

When she told her mother that she was off to the mall with Jody and that she wouldn't be home for dinner because she had a date, she got the reaction she expected. Her mother's lovely face glowed with satisfaction. "I'm so excited for you, honey. Your first dress-up date. Have you decided what you're going to wear?"

"Not really. What do you think?"

"I have just the thing. I forgot to give it to you earlier. Isn't it something? A real coincidence. I bought you a dress at Bloomingdale's yesterday. Let me get it now." She winked. "I'll hurry."

Angel waited in the kitchen, stunned by the realization that her mother had been thinking of her yesterday, had really cared enough to take the time to buy her a dress. She decided that if she ever thought her parents didn't love her, she would try and recall this moment.

Mom had always had excellent taste,

Angel thought, and she was prepared to like the dress simply because the lines and the material would be good. She wasn't prepared to love the dress so much, that she would shriek with pleasure when she saw it.

It was so perfect, and for a change, quite sophisticated. A heavy cotton cream-colored jersey, the dress had a V-neck and a slim skirt. The most stunning thing about it was the wide, Japanese-style sash in hot colors of pink, yellow, emerald green, and turquoise. In a small, plastic envelope, Angel found a pair of dangling turquoise earrings made to look like a bit of Japanese writing. "The sales lady told me that the character meant love," her mother said.

"I love *you*," Angel told her mother and nearly knocked her over with a giant hug. "Thank you, thank you, thank you. Thank Dad for me, too."

Red-faced from joy and running all the way to the corner, Angel grabbed Jody and hugged her, too. "What a day," she bubbled. "What a wonderful, gorgeous day. Guess what hapened, Jody? Everything — and, I mean everything is perfect. I can't believe the difference. Yesterday, the pits, today, heaven. Wait until I tell you."

"I'm waiting," Jody said, chuckling. "First though, calm yourself. You're frothing at the mouth."

All the way up to the mall, Angel talked. About the date with Jay. About her parents. About some of her doubts, too. Nothing incriminating, though. She told Jody that she had worried a lot because she had thought Jay liked her for the wrong reason.

Jody stared at her. "Clue me in. What's a wrong reason?"

"Oh, you know — I thought he liked me just for my looks, and I hate that. I really do, Jody."

"I'm confused, Angel. You mean that you'd be mad if you found out he thought you're pretty? I already told you that, don't you remember?"

"I know, but I mean *just* for that reason."

Jody sighed. They were at the front entrance to the mall.

"My advice is to stop thinking about it so much. So you're good-looking, what's the guy supposed to do? Not notice? Wear a blindfold? Or maybe you should consider reverse plastic surgery. Angel, you always worry too much."

That was true, Angel thought. Even Great Aunt Elizabeth had told her that she took life too seriously. Anyway, she wasn't going to spoil the day worrying about anything.

"Let's go to the bookstore first," Jody said. "You know how I love that place. Feel like browsing for a while, Angel? I hope?"

"What you love is the section on theater and films. I'll stick to fiction, but you can take all the time you want. So long as . . ." Angel grinned, ". . . we're home in time for me to get ready for you-know-who."

For the next half hour, Angel and Jody

browsed contentedly in separate sections of the large bookstore. By the time Jody joined Angel, they each had four paperbacks in their hands. Jody looked at the titles Angel had chosen. "I agree with every choice but one, Angel. Who is this author, Marietta Tindale? Never heard of her."

Jody took the book from Angel's pile, and flipped through the pages, then studied the back cover. "Doesn't sound too interesting to me. Who wants to read about some insecure girl who creeps around haunted houses, and lies to keep her family from knowing about her ghost boyfriend. Sounds like one of those stories where you hate the character for being such a dope, even though you're supposed to sympathize with her."

Angel reached for the book, and said lightly. "Did anyone ever tell you that you're a know-it-all, Jody?"

Jody grinned. "Don tells me that I'm a doll. Anyway, suit yourself. Buy the dumb book."

"It will be good. Tindale's books are *always* very good. I've read everything that she's written. This is her fifteenth, I think. She's won all kinds of awards, too. See, Jody? You don't always know it all."

Jody didn't seem to take offense. Instead, she reached for the book. "Let me see it again. I think you're wrong about the author, maybe, got her mixed up with someone else. I think it said on the back that this was her first novel."

"Forget it, Jody. I know I'm right. I told you, I've read all her other books."

As they waited in line at the register, Angel wondered why she'd make such a big deal about the book, why it had seemed so important, so necessary to argue with Jody about it. She'd never even heard of Marietta Tindale. It was such a dumb thing, and she felt drained and furious with herself.

While Jody was busy fishing in her shoulder bag for money to pay for her books, Angel quickly flipped the book over, and just as swiftly, read the blurb on the jacket. Jody was right. ". . . her first novel after twenty-five years as a journalist."

For the next two hours, Angel tried to be extra nice to Jody in order to make up for her nastiness in the bookstore. Not that Jody acted hurt or suspicious, but Angel was very aware that it would be easy enough for her friend to check out Marietta Tindale at the school library, or the next time she was at the bookstore. Finally, before she drove herself completely up the wall, Angel decided that she could say that after she'd read the book, she'd realized that it was Henrietta Tinsley she'd been thinking of.

Besides, Jody was much too excited about the beige wool jacket with slash pockets and standup collar to sense Angel's tenseness. When Jody finished putting the coat on layaway, they decided that they should head home.

Halfway home it started to pour. By the

time Angel reached her house, she was soaked through and through, her hair hanging like strands of a mop over her face. She was shivering, and her teeth were chattering. She only hoped that she wouldn't feel sick again. She couldn't stand it if anything spoiled the evening ahead.

Her parents were in the family room, and Angel could smell woodsmoke. She didn't go in to say hi because she knew her mother would complain about her being so wet and she would probably say: "You look like a drowned rat, Angel. Go do something with yourself."

Angel intended to do just that. A long, hot shower took away the chill, and by the time she was wrapped in her old terry robe, with a towel wrapped turban-style around her head, Angel could smile again. Her mother had put the new dress on a hanger, and hung it in her closet. Angel saw that her mother had selected shoes to go with the dress and put them on the closet floor directly under the dress. The beige heels were dainty but Angel had only worn them once and remembered that she had almost fallen twice. It wasn't going to happen tonight. The heels would be just fine.

She really enjoyed getting ready, and though she had plenty of time, she found herself getting nervous when she smudged the polish on her thumbnail for the second time.

Her hair acted spiteful, too, sticking out

at an odd angle on the left side. She'd had to wet it again and start over with the blow-dryer. But by six-fifteen, she was ready, and she went downstairs to wait for Jay.

Mom and Dad went a little crazy when they saw her, and Angel wished that they would stop fussing over her and sit down. Instead, she saw that her father had a camera in his hand.

"Please, Dad, no. And not when Jay comes either. He'll hate it."

Her father looked hurt. "Just one picture of you, then. I need a new one to show around, you know. The old one is falling to pieces from being passed around so much."

Angel groaned. She had always suspected that her father bragged about her to his co-workers, but she hated to think of strangers looking at her photo. "One picture, Dad, and please hurry before he comes."

When Jay rang the doorbell and she ushered him into the family room to meet her parents, she was quite certain that he couldn't tell that she had been a wreck only a minute before.

Her parents were fine. They didn't do anything to embarrass her, and they were friendly to Jay. They didn't say, "Get home early," or "Take care of our Angel."

Jay said that she was lucky to have such nice, super-attractive parents. "They're so proud of you, Angel. Easy to tell that."

He didn't know the half of it, Angel thought, and then forgot all about her mother and father when Jay helped her into an old but spotless blue sedan.

Before he started the car, he told her that he'd made reservations at the Wooden Nickel.

"Sound good to you?" he asked, then added, "You look so good tonight."

"You do, too. First time I've ever seen you with a tie."

She wished that he would stop staring at her like that.

"Shall we go, Jay? I can't wait to get there."

"Neither can I," Jay said softly, turning to put the keys in the ignition. "I can't wait to see you by candlelight. Okay, Angel, let's go. Consider us gone."

She laughed, and felt comfortable with him again.

Candlelight? Wait until she told Tania.

Nine

The Wooden Nickel was crowded. There were people lined up against the wall because every seat was taken. Jay led Angel by the hand to a small desk at the entrance to the dining room.

"I have reservations," Jay announced firmly to the smartly dressed man who stood scowling fiercely at a long list of names.

"Butler. Table for two."

The maitre d' looked up and studied Jay and Angel for a few seconds, then burst into a radiant smile. "My pleasure," he said, motioning for them to follow him and slipping two menus under his arm. He led them to a tiny table shoved close to what looked like an entire wall of movie screen.

"Woody Allen tonight," Jay said. "They told me when I called."

"Really? During dinner? What a great idea."

It would be great if making conversation turned out to be impossible.

One man brought a beverage list, and

asked if they would care for a drink before ordering. Jay looked at Angel, then ordered Cokes for them both. Another person in a red jacket brought rolls and butter, and poured ice water into their goblets.

Pretending to study the menu, Angel studied Jay instead. He looked wonderful she thought. His shoulders looked very wide under a navy blazer with gold buttons, white shirt, and a nice red, gray, and white striped tie. His hair looked nice, too, brushed sleekly against his tanned face. He didn't look seventeen at all — more like twenty-one, Angel decided. He had acted older, too. He seemed so confident and worldly, speaking to the maitre d' and even just sitting there scanning the menu.

Others had noticed him, too. Angel had seen many heads turn admiringly as they were led to their table. She had been pleased by all the attention Jay received and she hadn't been a bit sorry that no one bothered to look at her.

"I know what I want," Jay said. "Have you decided yet?"

"Not quite yet," Angel said and hid behind the menu. Luckily, the restaurant had included her very favorite foods, and it was easy. "I'm ready," she said, but before she laid the large menu down, she used it to sneak a fast glance around the dim and rather noisy restaurant. A few people were looking over at their table and Angel looked away quickly, embarrassed. A waiter was beside them with a pencil poised above a small pad.

"Chicken francaise and fettucine alfredo," she said firmly. "French dressing on my salad, and string beans, please."

Jay laughed softly. "I like a girl who knows her own mind. No doubts, no fuss." He looked up and winked at the waiter. "She knows my mind, too. I'll have the same."

"Really, Jay?" For some reason Angel was thrilled that their taste in food matched. "Great minds do think alike, I guess."

"Great taste buds in common," he said, and then spoiled it. "Jody's going to die of jealousy. Fettucine is her favorite food in the world."

Angel nodded, and took a sip of her water to stall. "Have you ever been here before?" *Who wants to talk about Jody on my first date,* she thought, smiling politely in Jay's direction.

"A few times," he said. "Way back. With my parents back in the good old days."

"Why good *old* days? Don't they take you out to dinner anymore?"

He shrugged and looked off into the distance above her head. Angel looked down at the tablecloth, at the next table, then back at Jay. She'd been imagining it, she decided. He hadn't given her a dirty look, then looked away, disgusted.

Another young man came and lit the candle under the glass. When the red glass globe was replaced, the flickering light sent red shadows into the hollows under Jay's eyes and cheekbones and around his mouth. Angel stared, thinking that he looked lean and hungry and much, much older.

Jay caught her staring, but at that moment the waiter began setting out their food. There were so many plates, saucers, and bowls that they both laughed. Angel wondered if the tiny table would collapse from the weight of their meal. It looked delicious. She couldn't wait to eat it.

"If you could see your face, Angel," Jay said as soon as the waiter was gone. "I wasn't sure if you could wait until he put the food down. You look . . ." he laughed, ". . . ready to attack."

Angel couldn't answer him because she was already chewing tender chicken with a creamy, lemony sauce. It was delicious, but she couldn't wait to taste the fettucine.

It was funny though, she thought. He was the one who had looked so gaunt and starving in the red candlelight.

At least five minutes went by before they spoke again, except for appreciative murmurs, and broken phrases like: "Good . . . very" or "This . . . fabulous."

Finally Angel put her fork down. She dabbed at her mouth with a blue linen napkin. "Not another bite or I'll bust." Immediately she was embarrassed. She wished she hadn't said something so childish.

"Me, too," Jay said, taking one more bite. After a minute he told her, "Better watch it, Angel. We've just had the most fattening food in the place."

She made a face. Did he have to say *that?*

"You remind me of my mother and father. They're my weight-watchers. They monitor every bite I take."

Jay looked shocked. "How come? I mean, you're far from fat. Angel, hey, did they make you go on that fast?"

She paused. "They didn't make me, no, but. . . ."

Jay was leaning toward her, waiting, his eyes dark and full of concern. "But what?"

"They just suggested it. They gave me the magazine and told me to read the article."

She was suddenly horrified and so, it appeared, was Jay. But it was too late now. She had to say something. "You see, Jay, my parents think I should be perfect. At least, on the outside. That's all they really care about — how I look. I don't think that they have any idea what goes on inside me."

She paused, feeling guilty, thinking of how sweet her mother and father had been that day. "Usually, they're too busy with each other to notice me."

"Is that the story of your life?" Jay asked softly. "No one understands you at home?" He laughed harshly. "Join the club."

"You, too?" Angel asked, surprised.

"Never mind me for now. You're the one who looks sad here."

"Maybe," Angel said. "But I really don't know anything about you, Jay, and I'd like to." *I'd like to know a little more than Jody does, if that's possible,* Angel thought.

"Not much to tell. Dad is a supervisor at Schweitzer's. Michelle is six, Matthew is eight. Mom used to work at the mall, but she doesn't now. I'm seventeen, almost eighteen. My middle name is Lansing, and I have grandparents in New England. I like food, and most recently, acting, and a girl named Angel. Your turn."

"Oh, Jay. Not like that. I didn't mean . . . facts."

"What, then?" Angel thought he looked embarrassed for the first time all evening. "You wanted to know about me."

"Not *about* you, Jay. Jody could tell me *about* you. I want to know . . . how you feel about things."

"Aha. Feelings, no facts. I see."

The waiter was back, hovering and smiling, wanting to know if they wanted dessert. Angel shook her head emphatically.

"Two coffees, and the check."

Angel wondered how many guys at Edgemont High would be so smooth and at ease.

Somehow he managed not to return to the subject and Angel didn't push it. Just as the waiter brought the check the lights dimmed further and Woody Allen in a bulky white space suit came to huge life at Angel's right. She jumped and Jay cracked up. "Get away from my girl, Woody," he growled playfully.

"Bad timing," he said. "Movietime just when we're finished. Oh, well, there's sup-

104

posed to be a band upstairs. We can dance."

"Great," she said, liking it that he held her hand as they left the dining room and climbed the wide, carpeted flight of stairs to the Parlour where a poster announced "Music To Make You Remember — Packy Winston and His Sweet Talkers, Oldies but Goodies."

"Oh, *no*," Jay groaned. "I'm messing up but good tonight. I forget to ask what time they show the movie, and I also forget to ask what kind of music. . . . Oldies, but goodies. Sorry, Angel."

She squeezed his hand hard. "Don't be sorry. In fact, I'll probably recognize the songs. My parents are always playing old albums. Let's dance, Jay. Come on."

It took a few minutes to get used to each other and the rhythm, but soon they were doing fine, even imitating the dips and turns of some of the middle-aged couples. The soft pressure of his hand against her back, the butterfly tickle of his lips against her brow felt new and exciting, but familiar and comforting at the same time. Slow-dancing was not something Angel had done often, but with Jay it was so easy and fun.

"We're good together, aren't we?" he said while they waited for another song to begin. "And I was so afraid I was going to destroy your feet."

They danced for a long time, until her high heels began to hurt her feet. They sat down, and Jay ordered them each a Coke, but they couldn't talk over the music. They danced one last time to "Somewhere over the Rainbow"' and then Jay looked at his watch.

"Angel, we'd better go. I have to get the car home by midnight. Usually it's the girl who has a curfew. Sorry."

"Please stop saying that," Angel said. "You don't have to apologize to me."

He opened the passenger door of the car. "Sure, okay. But after tonight I *know* how lucky I am. Every guy in the place wished he were me, Angel."

"What are you *talking about*?" She had to repeat her question because he had shut her door and gone around to the driver's side. When he got in, she stopped him from putting the key in the ignition. "Wait. What did you mean . . . guys were wishing they were you?"

"Oh, Angel. You must have seen everyone staring at you when we walked in. And when we were dancing, too."

She looked at him wide-eyed, and sighed. "I didn't notice."

He started the car, and backed up, using the rearview mirror and leaning slightly against Angel. "Okay, but I felt really good. After all, I was the one you were with. You must be used to it by now. With your looks, Angel, you should be."

That's the wrong kind of attention but he's not going to understand that, Angel thought wearily. "Sure, Jay."

They didn't talk very much on the way, but Jay punched in a music station on the FM radio. She sat close enough to Jay to feel his warmth and smell the spicy aftershave, and she let the music wash over her. Drowsy, Angel moved closer and rested her head on his shoulder.

"Mmmm, nice," he whispered. "An angel on my shoulder."

"Your guardian angel?" she asked sleepily.

"My gorgeous angel."

"*Oh, Jay.*" Angel sat up fast and stared grimly through the side window. "Is that the reason you wanted to take me out? Because you think I'm gorgeous and you want to show me off?"

Incredibly he laughed. He didn't sound upset at all.

"It's one of the reasons, sure. I *love* to look at you. Is there anything wrong with that? It's not the only reason, okay? In case, you're wondering, I like you a lot. Okay, Angel?"

In a way, there was nothing wrong with it. "Okay, Jay. Sorry. I shouldn't have jumped on you like that. It's just that I get so ... hey, are we *home*? We're at *my* house?"

Jay put the car in gear, and turned sideways in the seat. He was looking at her.

"Do angels ever kiss, I wonder?" His voice was low, and teasing. "Or do they just float around playing the harp and singing hallelujah?"

"I don't know," she whispered. What was she supposed to say? She wanted Jay to kiss her so much, but she could only peer into those shadowed eyes and wait. She wondered frantically if she was supposed to move closer to let him know it was all right to kiss her or . . . what? "Jay?"

Suddenly his arms were around her and his lips were pressing against hers, firm and warm and wonderful.

When the kiss ended, Jay whispered something, but whatever he said was lost in the moment.

"I had a wonderful time," Angel whispered. "Thank you."

"I'll walk you to the door," he said, and in a minute she was out of the car and they were walking hand in hand up her front steps.

"Thank you," she said again, and he bent and kissed her on the tip of her nose.

"You're welcome."

Once inside her house Angel went into the dark living room and from the bay window watched the tail lights of the blue car disappear into the darkness. Very softly Angel sang out, "Hallelujah."

She went upstairs carrying a beige highheeled shoe in each hand, and when she was at the top step, heard: "Angel? Is that you? Did you have a good time?"

Mom was standing in the doorway of her bedroom with a book in her hand. Her reading glasses had been pushed up on top of her hair. She put a cautioning finger to her lips. "Your father's asleep."

"A great time, Mom. Thanks."

"Good-night, Angel."

Angel wasn't tired, but after she'd hung up the new dress, put the shoes on the rack, and put on her pajamas, she got into bed and pulled the covers up. *I might as well be warm while I think. I'll leave the light on in case I want to read.*

Angel expected to stay awake for at least an hour while she reviewed her date with Jay and tried to figure out why her mother and father had changed overnight.

She fell asleep with the light on.

*T*en

For the next three weeks Angel was busier and happier than she'd been in months, maybe even years. For as long as she could remember, she had *never* been completely happy.

And now I am, she thought, halfway through typing the lyrics for "Danny, My Love." The job of typing and copying the words to every song was hers, and for the first few pages she'd stayed after school and used the business lab's electric typewriters. She eventually gave up, went home, and took her typewriter — a hand-me-down manual from her mother — and set up shop at the kitchen table. Angel had learned to type on the small, battered machine, and now it was almost dancing off the table under her furious fingers.

"You'll have to move, Angel. I can't have that mess on the table while I'm trying to make dinner. And you know that your father likes to keep me company and make the salad."

Her mother stared at her critically, then gestured for Angel to push the hair out of her eyes.

"Tonight we're having fettucine and your father is in charge, as usual. I know you're happy about that, so go now, and take all this debris with you. Angel, can't you do anything without chaos? I can't even step in that room of yours. It's full of sawdust."

Her mother was picking papers off the table at random and piling them together. *"Hey, stop,* Mom. You're mixing them all up. They're all collated . . . it's supposed to be —"

"Upstairs. So I can wipe off the table. And before you come down, Angel, please do something with your hair and face. You've got carbon all over you."

I was happy, Angel thought, clamping her lips together so she wouldn't give in to the impulse to scream long and loud. *I am happy,* she decided, *just not at home.* She could think of only a small revenge.

"I don't think I can eat fettucine tonight. I've had it three times since the last time Dad made it. At the Wooden Nickel, at Archer's Deli, and over at Jay's house. His mother is such a great gourmet cook."

Mom looked sour. "Fettucine is the most fattening dish in the world. I guess I'll tell your father not to bother, then. Angel, I didn't know that you'd been to Jay's home. You didn't tell me. And what's this about Archer's Deli? They don't serve anything but hamburgers and sub sandwiches."

Angel lifted the heavy typewriter, then looked at the pile of papers. "Mom, would you put those on top, please? Here, right under my chin. Thanks." The typewriter was tight against her chest, the papers wedged under her chin. It was impossible to say her words dramatically without the proper gestures. She settled for soft and wistful.

"The Archers make it for me special . . . anytime I want. Flo says she'd give her right arm to have a daughter just like me." Angel was halfway out the door into the hall, but she added, "They're such sweet people. I just love them."

Angel went upstairs on a rush of adrenalin, but her triumph ended when she put the typewriter down on her bureau. The typewritten lyrics floated to the floor, and she sank down on her knees to retrieve them. Mom had looked stricken, she thought. Angel thought maybe the crack about Flo Archer's right arm was too obvious, and it *was* cruel to say that she loved the deli owners. It was hard to say "I love you" to her own parents and she rarely did. Certainly not lately. Angel had always blamed that on her parents because they didn't say "I love you" often either. At least not to her. But Angel was absolutely sure that her mother and father told each other those three important words every day. Her father whispered something to her mother and kissed her whenever he left the house. Angel's kisses were usually blown at her as he ran out the front door.

That didn't matter so much anymore, Angel decided, scanning the page of lyrics in her hand. It was "You're the One That I Want" — Sandy and Danny's big duet. She sang it softly to herself, and for the very first time, she wished that she was an actress like Jody and Tania. Singing to Danny . . . Jay. Jay . . . Danny singing to her Onstage with everyone watching. The fantasy ended abruptly when Angel spotted one error after another. She would have to type it over, she thought, remembering that Mr. Damian was soon going to announce extra rehearsals that would be devoted to learning these songs.

She carried the typewriter over to her desk and set it down on the shiny, new surface. At least she'd done something right; the finish was flawless, the wood stain even and rich. Too bad she didn't have time to finish the end tables, but there had been so many other things to do.

Angel worked on the programs during study hall, and got Tania and Jody to help her scout for props and the hard-to-find items, and post 3 x 5 cards on the bulletin board asking for donations. Mr. James, as usual, was Angel's best source for donations, and she promised that his name would appear on the program.

Jay helped, too. It was his idea to substitute pink T-shirts for the expensive pink satin jackets worn by the girls in the movie. He made a special trip to the mall to get an estimate. There were a dozen "Pink Ladies," so the cost of T-shirts was going to come out of the drama club treasury. Angel was impressed with how willing he was to help the production and her.

Jay was her boyfriend now, no doubt about that. Since that first date, Angel could count three more. She wasn't even adding the afternoons at Archer's Deli, or walking home together after rehearsal. It was getting too cold to do that much longer, and Angel supposed that Jay would go straight home instead of stopping for a snack at her house.

Twice they had gone to the movies, and once, roller-skating, but not over to Jay's house. Angel hadn't even met his family yet. She wanted to ask Jay if Jody was over at his house a lot, but she never dared. The truth was, she didn't want to know.

Sometimes, though not every night, Jay phoned and they talked. He never seemed to like to stay on the phone. That bothered her, too, although at school he was always there for her, waiting after class to walk with her and sitting next to her at lunch and always, *always* looking at her as if she were his favorite candy. He was always taking inventory, always admiring her voice, her hair, her walk, and her smile. He loved her eyes, he said, and named them "Summer Blue." Angel tried not to mind but she did. A lot.

"Jay's been practicing his guitar," Jody

said one day, "for the hayride. Don's going to bring his ukulele. I can't wait, can you, Angel?"

Angel tried to look enthusiastic. Jay hadn't ever mentioned the guitar. He'd never told her that he could play at all. She didn't say that to Jody.

A few more times Jody spilled out other facts about Jay. Nothing terribly important, but Angel began to avoid Jody whenever possible. They were still best friends, but Angel found it harder and harder to listen to her talk about Jay.

Still, even with those small hurts and pangs, the past three weeks had been very good. She'd lost count of how many times Jay had kissed her, but it was somewhere between six and eight.

At dinner, Angel had to look away from the creamy noodles, but the smell of butter, parmesan cheese, and cream was torture.

"Too bad you can't eat Dad's fettucine, Angel. I hate to see it go to waste."

Angel closed her eyes tightly, then opened them fast, trying to blink away the image of the flat noodles sliding into the garbage disposal. "Mmmm, too bad," Angel muttered.

"Rehearsal again tonight, Angel?" Dad asked.

"Yes," she said. "Mr. Damian gets nervous, and so he overdoes it." Angel was glad, though. Rehearsals were better than staying home with the Siamese twins.

Dad offered to drop her off at school, and

Angel was shocked until he explained that he had to go to the drugstore anyway. She called Tania to let her know that she wouldn't need a ride. When Angel arrived, Don and Jay were sitting on the edge of the stage, their long legs dangling.

"Early birds," Angel said, joining them. "What's up?"

"I've been telling Jay that I plan to lock him in the utility closet on opening night. My mother is telling me that I have star quality, so I thought . . ." The red-headed boy grinned slyly.

"Think again, Kiernan," Jay said, affecting a Danny Zuko pose. "Don't believe everything your mother tells you. After all, you're my number two understudy. Steve was good, but I don't know about you, Don."

Don was suddenly serious. "Anyone know what that story is? It wasn't like Steve to just quit like that. Talk about a Goody-Two-Shoes conscientious person — he was *it*. I haven't even seen him around, have you?"

Jay shook his head. "I haven't either. Someone told me that he hadn't been in school for over a week then came back and wouldn't answer any questions. He was a clam."

Angel said nothing. She didn't want to think about Steve Ellis. She also wished that Don and Jay would change the subject. She tried. "Tania's terrific as Frenchy, isn't she? She makes me laugh when she chews her bubble gum so hard."

During the week, Tania put her heart and soul into the role. She even practiced being Frenchy in the cafeteria, cracking up everyone in the area. She told Angel and Jody she already had one great outfit: white pedal pushers, a purple sweater with a cinch belt, and black pumps. She was going to wear gobs of makeup, and her hair would be fluffed up and curled under. She didn't go anywhere without her script. Frenchy was cute in a tough way, a wisecracker with a heart that was big, and a brain that was a bit too small. Tania was never sharp-tongued like the character she played, but like Frenchy, she always had a funny crack, or a story to tell. Angel knew that all of her stories were true, though. If they weren't, Tania told you so.

When Jody arrived, Jay jumped over the stage and walked over to meet her. Angel stood on the stage and watched, hating herself for being jealous and resentful. It was stupid to imagine that something was wrong with their talking together, laughing together. Only Jay didn't look as if he were laughing. In profile, he seemed very tense and talkative. Angel saw Jody listening intently, then saying something that he obviously didn't like. She saw Jay shake his head repeatedly, and read his lips. "No," he said. "No way."

What on earth were they talking about?

It wasn't easy to pretend that she didn't feel resentful. Fortunately, Jody didn't seem to notice, and Jay became engrossed in touching up the Chevy with red paint. The car was the main attraction for the guys at the moment. Even without their leather jackets, Angel thought they looked like T-Birds already.

During break, Angel had to answer some questions from her building crew. Afterward she wandered back to the lounge looking for Jay. He was there with Jody. There were a few other kids in the room, but they had their own conversation going. Jody and Jay were talking, and Angel thought that they both looked depressed.

Angel went over to the soda machine and dropped change in the slot. "What's up, you two?" she asked carefully. "Did someone *die*?"

Jay's head shot up and he glared at her. His hazel eyes were very green, Angel noticed. "Not funny, Angel," he said.

Angel looked from Jody to Jay. "So tell me? What's the matter?"

"Oh, nothing much. Just some . . . problems," answered Jay.

Angel sat down beside Jay and put her hand on his arm. She suddenly felt very ashamed of herself. As his girl, it was her place to comfort him. "Can I help?"

"Not really. It's just family stuff."

Angel was puzzled. "What kind of stuff?"

"It's just that I probably won't make the next couple of rehearsals. Mom's going . . ."

She was instantly sympathetic. "Oh, Jay, that's too bad. She's sick again, huh? And you have to watch the kids. Listen, don't worry. I'll get all the song lyrics to you tonight and you can practice on Michelle and Matthew. Mr. Damian can't complain too much if you're doing something."

"Okay, thanks," Jay said, glancing at Jody. "One other thing though. I won't be able to ... I mean, I have to break our date for tomorrow night."

Angel stared at him, then smiled. "I won't let you. Tell you what, Jay. I'll come over and help you babysit."

There was such a long silence and Angel suddenly felt very self-conscious. And another feeling, that she knew very well, was hitting her hard. She felt left out, an extra, an unnecessary third person. "Forget it," she said sharply. "It was a bad idea."

"No, it wasn't," Jay said gently, then sighing dejectedly. "It's just that my mother wouldn't want anyone in the house when she's sick."

Angel knew that Jay had meant "a stranger" when he said "anyone." Mrs. Butler probably wouldn't mind if Jody came over. "Okay, don't worry about it. Just practice those songs. Mr. Damian has some tapes, too, and I'm sure he'll let you borrow them."

The rest of the rehearsal seemed to drag. Mr. Damian was in a somber mood, and so he didn't make any of the actors miserable with his demands. Angel was glad when it was over and she could go home. It didn't really surprise her when Jay said that he was going straight home. It was too cold to walk; sunny October had turned into a wet, bone-chilling November.

The next night, Friday, Angel stayed home. Tania was going to Staten Island the next morning and she wanted to get lots of "beauty sleep." Jody was going out to dinner with her mother and her aunt. Angel kept hoping that Jody would ask her to join them. When she didn't, it seemed like a sign that Jody didn't care about her anymore. Jody was still her bouncy, bubbly, affectionate self, but still Angel wondered.

"Call me in the morning, Angel. Not too early. We'll think of something to do."

Several times in the evening, Angel had to talk herself out of calling Jay. She wished that he would call her and at least say hi, or something to let her know that he was thinking of her. The phone didn't ring. Mom and Dad had gone to a card party. There was nothing good on TV, so she ended up taking a bath and painting her toenails. Then she finished the last three chapters of *Catcher in the Rye*.

At 10:35 the phone rang shrilly, and Angel almost fell over her feet in her hurry to answer it. She sighed in happy relief when she heard Jay's voice.

"Just wanted to say hi," he said, and Angel smiled at herself in the mirror over the phone table. Wishes did come true, she thought. "I miss you, Angel."

She was happy again, and happier still when he sang a few bars of Danny's part in the duet with Sandy. "You're the One That I Want" was the biggest song in the show. Angel even found herself getting breathless when he sang — Danny-style — "I've got chills . . . they're multiplying . . . I'm losing control. For the power you're supplying . . . is electrifying."

Jay didn't know all the words yet, but it had sounded great to Angel, anyway. He was going to be wonderful as Danny.

"You've got one big fan," she said softly. *"Me."*

Her expression changed drastically when Jay said, "Jody just left. She stopped by when she got back from having dinner. The song sounded better when I did it with her.

"I'd better go. My father's on second shift and he might be trying to use the line. Call you tomorrow, Angel."

Angel waited several seconds after she hung up, and picked up the phone again. She dialed Jody's number, and then Jay's.

They were both still busy even after ten minutes. She tried their numbers six times altogether.

Angel didn't believe for a moment that Jay's father was on the line. It was Jody and Jay talking about things that apparently they didn't want Angel to know about.

She had chills now — apprehension — and her bad feelings were multiplying. She was definitely in danger of losing control.

*E*leven

At eleven on Saturday morning, Angel picked up the phone and called Jody. She'd thought about this call carefully, planning her words while she sanded the top of an end table. She was sure she wouldn't be nervous, but as she waited for Jody to pick up the phone on her end, Angel's hands were shaking.

"Oh, good, it's you, Angel. Did you think of something to do? We shouldn't waste a Saturday."

We shouldn't, but I sometimes have to, Angel thought bitterly, remembering the miserable few hours she'd wasted in the mall a few weeks ago. "It's going to rain or snow, Jody. The weatherman was playing it safe, I guess. I think I should stay in and work on my room. I don't have too much left to do."

Angel didn't think her friend sounded very disappointed.

"If you're going to do that, Angel, maybe I'll do something about my pit of a room.

It's really bad — well, *you* know. My mom isn't screaming yet, but she's about to, I think. Maybe you can come over later and check it out, okay?"

"Maybe. I'll see how much I get done." Angel clutched the phone tighter. "Hey, Jody, I need your advice."

"Sure, Angel," Jody said, her voice taking on a tone of warm concern. "I'm always there for you, you know that."

"It's just that I'm not sure . . . how to . . ." Angel's mouth was bone dry. The words weren't coming easily yet. ". . . how to help Jay. With his mom, I mean. I know how hard it is for him, having to babysit all the time, cooking meals. He won't let me help him, Jody, and I want to."

Angel had thought if she was general . . . humble enough, Jody might open up and tell her what was going on. Angel didn't really care to know about his family life as much as she wanted to find out why he wouldn't confide in her. Suddenly she had a terrible thought — what if Jay's mother was dying? Maybe that would explain why he talked to Jody. After all, their families were close friends and neighbors.

Angel took a deep breath. "I just wish I could make him happier, Jody. Sometimes he talks about it, but not very often. He said that he didn't want to burden me, but that's not right — I'm his *girl*, Jody." She hesitated. "I know he has you to talk to. It's good but . . . Jody? Will you tell me something? What does he say to you about it? All he says to me is . . . well, you know . . . the basics."

If Angel had been telling the truth, the sentence would have been: "He doesn't say anything to me."

"Oh, Angel. Don't worry so much. It's just that Jay is a very private person and it's hard for him to talk about his mother's problem. He must really like and trust you a lot to tell you *anything* about it. He's so protective of his mother and his father and the kids, too. A great guy, really, but a little too proud."

Angel was staring up at the ceiling. "I know what you mean, Jody. Anyway, how is Mrs. Butler doing? Is her problem getting better?"

Easy now, Angel thought. *Be careful, because you're getting very close.* Jay said that his mother was sick; what was this about a problem? She would find out any minute if she was clever and asked the right questions.

"She's doing just great," Jody said enthusiastically. "Jay says she calls home every night after supper and talks to him and the kids. It's so great that she's there, finally. It took courage, but I'll bet you she'll make it."

"I don't know her," Angel said. "But Jay seems to think that —"

Jody interrupted in a slightly angry voice. "Jay is too much of a pessimist. He doesn't really understand alcoholism. He thinks because an alcoholic can't be cured and is always considered to be recovering, that there's no hope. But it's not true. Haviland House has a great program. Jay and I — we argue a lot about it. He gets so mad at me. But if you want to help, just keep on being yourself. Jay is crazy about you, you know." She chuckled. "I *hope* you know."

"I know," Angel said faintly. In a way, she was sorry she ever asked. For one thing, Jay hadn't trusted her enough, and for a second thing, she knew that she had lied her way into finding out about a family problem that was none of her business. If Jay ever found out that she'd pried the information from Jody . . . Angel wasn't going to think about that.

"How long will she be at Haviland House?"

"Eight weeks. In two weeks she can come home on weekends."

Angel groaned. For the next several weeks Jay was going to be very unreliable. While his father was at work, Jay would have full charge of the house and kids. Angel wanted to help, but if he didn't tell her, what could she do? It was very obvious that he needed Jody's shoulder to cry on.

"Mr. Damian is going to have a fit. I hope Jay will explain it to him."

"Don't hold your breath, Angel," Jody said wryly. "Jay isn't about to broadcast his personal problems to anyone. He's as stubborn as . . . well, he's stubborn, Angel. You've probably seen examples of that by now."

"Oh, sure," Angel said, frowning. "He's wonderful though, don't you think so, Jody?" She was surprised by how much she wanted to know Jody's response. She wasn't sure that Jody could answer without admitting that Jay was more than just a friend.

"Wonderful?" she laughed. "I wouldn't go *that* far. I know him too well. How can you praise a person that you've seen in training pants? Who you've seen act like a brat too many times? Who you used to beat up? I stole Jay's sandbox shovel, and he'll never let me forget it."

Angel didn't believe her. She was too light about him, too cute. She wanted to get off the phone, stop listening and start digesting what she'd learned.

"I'll try to be supportive, I guess. I mean, *more* supportive. Jody, please don't mention to Jay that we were talking about him. Jody, you helped . . . just talking about it. It's our secret, okay?"

"Sure thing," Jody said easily. "And now to the Room of Horrors. Call me later, Angel."

Angel paced around her room until she heard a knock at the door. It was her mother. "Just wanted to tell you that we're off to the mall." She peered at Angel and frowned. "If you want to come with us, get ready. We're leaving in five minutes. Your father and I were thinking of having lunch at Victoria Station after we finished our shopping."

Angel looked out the window. "You and

Dad go ahead. I planned to work on the tables this afternoon. I'll make a sandwich later." She glanced at her mother and sighed. "Don't worry, I'm also planning to brush my hair."

Pacing, Angel had repeatedly dragged her fingers through her long hair. It usually helped her to think, but from the expression on her mother's face, Angel knew that the gesture hadn't done much for her appearance.

Mom's clouded face cleared. "That's my girl."

Angel muttered under her breath when her mother left the room, "Since when?"

About three o'clock the phone rang, and with an oak-stained hand Angel picked it up on the fourth ring. It was Jay, and he sounded happy — his sense of humor seemed to be in full gear. He sang "Greased Lightenin' " for her, and told her three jokes. He asked her if she wanted to go out. "Who knows where? Maybe the movies, although I don't know what's playing. Do you have a paper?"

"We don't have to go anywhere," Angel said. "If you want, you can come over here and we'll find a good movie on cable. I'll even make popcorn."

"Sounds great, Pretty Angel. I'll be over after I give the kids supper."

"Good. I'll see you whenever. 'Bye, Jay." There was no more mystery. Angel guessed that Mr. Butler must be home to babysit.

Mom and Dad had invited two couples over to play cards, but they didn't seem to mind that she'd invited Jay. They were going to use the dining room table, anyway. Angel could use the family room, and, according to Dad, there would be nonstop popcorn for everyone.

Angel had a great fire going when Jay arrived, and in a matter of minutes they were sitting crosslegged with their backs to the leaping flames, watching *Stripes*. Jay was thrilled. He said he'd seen the movie four times already, but he could see it a dozen more. Bill Murray was a riot. Jay sent Angel into laughing fits when he imitated a few of the characters. He *did* know how to act, Angel thought, holding her sides.

All in all, it was a fun evening, and Jay's kiss when he said good-night was especially long and tender.

"I think I love you, Angel Porter," he whispered.

"Oh, Jay, I love you, too," she whispered back, then hugged him tight.

When he was gone, Angel helped her parents clean up. Her father even said that he liked her choice in boyfriends, and her mother smiled and said that she agreed wholeheartedly.

"Jay is quite handsome," she added, and patted Angel on the back. "Both of you have excellent taste."

It didn't ruin Angel's mood at all. No matter what her parents did, she had Jay now. They loved each other.

Just as Angel was climbing the stairs, her mother called to her. "Did Jay tell you that I invited him to dinner tomorrow?"

Angel halted and called back. "No, he didn't. Is he coming?"

Mom walked into the hall and looked up at her. "No, he said he had to cook dinner for his brother and sister. I thought it was sort of strange. Didn't you tell me that his mother is a fabulous cook?"

Angel stared at her mother. "She is. It's just that she hasn't been feeling well."

"That's too bad. What's wrong with her?"

"I'm not sure. Jay didn't tell me."

Her mother shook her head. "I certainly hope it's nothing serious."

"I don't know, Mom. Jay's kind of close-mouthed about his . . . personal life."

Mom laughed and headed back to the kitchen. "I thought *you* were his personal life, Angel. He adores you, I can tell."

"Mmmm, I guess," Angel said, and continued up the stairs.

If Jay adored her, she had nothing to worry about. Jody wasn't going to say anything, no matter what. Angel loved her friend for that.

At seven o'clock on Sunday night, Angel was watching *60 Minutes* on TV. Her mother and father were cuddled up on the couch, and, Angel, could see, that they weren't too far from sleep. Seven o'clock! She was sure that she was going to be downstairs by herself all evening, unless she went to bed early, too.

She was restless. No special reason that she could think of, but she just couldn't seem to sit still. Her mother would call her "fidgety," or "antsy." Angel switched the channels, then turned it back to channel two and tried to concentrate on the interview of some dishonest politician who was protesting going to jail.

She thought about calling Tania, but she didn't. Anyway, she probably wasn't back from Staten Island yet. Angel had no desire to talk to Jody. She felt uneasy about their conversation the day before. She knew she was worrying for no reason, but she was nervous — her feet wouldn't stay still. She would get a snack and a glass of milk. Not that she was so hungry, but it would give her something to do. Maybe she *was* hungry? Her stomach — her entire insides — felt upset.

At seven-thirty the doorbell rang. Angel looked over and saw that her parents were out like twin lights. She went to the door, and before opening it, looked out through the glass side panel. Jay was standing there, but his head was bent slightly as if he were staring at his shoes.

"Jay. Hey, nice surprise." She was so happy to see him.

She held the door open, smiling, but when he looked up, Angel's eyes widened. She'd seen him look angry twice before. The first time was when the school office personnel had bugged him about being late to school, and made him feel like a little kid. The second time when he was mad at Mr. Damian.

This time was worse. Jay looked ready to blow his top. "What's the matter?" she asked uncertainly. "You're . . . you're upset."

He walked past her into the hall, and continued into the family room. Angel guessed that he spotted her parents sleeping on the couch, because he turned around fast and walked back to her. "How about the kitchen?" he said evenly. "I need to talk to you, Angel."

"Sure. Sure, Jay, follow me."

Something must have happened at home. Angel wondered if maybe it had something to do with his mother suddenly not doing so well. Maybe she was home and drinking again. She didn't blame Jay for being angry after all he'd been through.

The truth is I don't even know what he's been through, Angel thought. It frightened her to think that she wasn't even able to tell the difference between her lies and her truths.

Jay leaned against the dishwasher, and, looking at his face, Angel pulled out a chair and sat facing him.

"Tell me, Jay. I'll help if I can."

"I hope so," he said. "I really do hope so, Angel."

Jay's shoulders were hunched forward, and he kept clenching and unclenching his fists. She saw perspiration on his upper lip. *Had he run all the way to her house?* she wondered.

"Who told you about my mother? Jody said you already knew about it. . . . I mean, about my mom's problem. Something's not right. Jody said that *you* said that *I* told you. We both know that I didn't tell you anything, so who was it, huh?"

His eyes were narrowed; and Angel wanted to run as fast as she could away from his accusing eyes and words. He was steaming. "I *said*, I want to know who told you, Angel. *Please*."

Less than twenty-four hours ago, Jay had put his arms around her, kissed her, and said, "I think I love you." She wanted to cry. What could she do to make the anger go away.

"Jay, I don't want to make any trouble. You and Jody have been friends for too long."

Jay stood up straight. "What are you talking about?" His eyes seemed to drill into her mind. Frightened, she wondered, if he could read her thoughts.

"Well, I told Jody that I'd keep it secret. You know, Jay, we are best friends."

"Angel, please. Just spill it."

"I was talking to Jody yesterday, and I said that I wished your mother would get well. I didn't ask what was wrong with her. That's when she said that from what I'd said, she thought I probably didn't know what kind of sickness your mother has."

Angel's blue eyes pleaded with his hazel ones. "So I said I didn't and . . . she told me. Your mom's at Haviland House, and that's why you had to break our date Friday."

Jay winced, as if she'd just thrown something in his face.

"Did Jody fill you in on all the details? Did she tell you what Mom was like before?" He pounded his fist into the palm of his other hand. "I can't believe she did it. Jody is . . . I mean, I've trusted her with everything that's ever happened to me."

A sense of disgust was growing in her mind. Angel couldn't believe that she was doing this to Jody. Like always, she allowed the words to come out smoothly and skillfully. Angel thought that all her childhood stories, all the times she had embroidered the truth with extra little details — the tiny fibs and the large ones — had given her an actress' polish to the lines she spoke. *Oh, Jody, I'm sorry. I wish I didn't have to do this.*

"Jay, she really didn't mean any harm. I mean, she just thought I should know because you and I are going out. As far as I know, she hasn't told anyone but me."

"That's nice," Jay said sarcastically. "Every bit of loyalty helps."

"Don't be mad at her, Jay. And, please,

133

please don't tell Jody that I told you."

"Why not?" Jay looked puzzled. "I'm going to straighten her out as soon as I leave here."

"No, please don't tell her. I promised her, Jay. After she told me, she said she felt bad about betraying your confidence in her. I told her I wouldn't tell you it was her. I made a solemn vow."

He was looking at her so skeptically. *"Come on,* Angel. You don't owe her that."

Angel closed her eyes tightly. A part of her seemed to be standing off to one side, shaking her head in bewilderment and also, contempt. Bit by bit, word by word, she was weaving her most awful lie yet. She felt sick to her stomach.

"Yes, I do. Just forget it, can't you? Don't say anything to her at all. And if you want . . . if you need to talk to someone. . . ."

The other Angel hung her head in shame. ". . . you can talk to me."

"Ah, Angel, thanks." Jay put his arms around her as she sat in the chair, and she was very still, breathing in the fresh air and shampoo scent of him. His face rested on her shoulder and she could hear his ragged breathing. Finally, he lifted his head and looked into her eyes.

"At least I have you, Angel. I can trust you, can't I?"

"Yes," she said harshly, then held up her mouth for his kiss. Her answer wasn't a lie, she thought wildly. She would never again say anything or do anything to hurt him.

He straightened but he kept his hands on her shoulders. He sighed deeply, then took her shoulders and shook her slightly.

"Don't ever do what Jody did, please."

"I won't. You're not going to say anything to her, are you?"

"No, Angel. I'm going to go home now and sack out. I hope my father has the kids in bed early." He grinned bravely. "I've had it with *Candyland* and *Trouble*.

Angel forced a smile. She'd had it with trouble for sure.

"I love you, Jay. And stop worrying."

"Love you, too. Consider me not worried. I'll see you at the corner in the morning."

She watched him jogging down the street and she walked over to the cream velvet loveseat and sank down. She wrapped her arms around herself and hugged tight.

She felt sick and empty, and incredibly ugly. *Consider me very worried*, she thought gloomily. She truly was.

Twelve

One more lie wasn't going to make a big difference. Angel told her mother that her throat was sore, closed her bedroom door, and went back to sleep for an hour. When she woke up, the house was quiet except for the tap-tap-tap of Mom's fingers on the typewriter.

Angel wandered downstairs in slippers and robe, but her mother didn't even look up. For a minute or two, Angel stood in the doorway of the den and tried to work up enough courage to ask her mother if she would put aside her work for a little while because she needed to talk to her.

It was a bad idea. Angel saw the stack of papers and folders on the desk beside the typewriter, and realized that she'd never be able to hold her mother's attention. Dad, Harvest Foods, top priorities. Then — maybe — her daughter.

Angel went to the kitchen, filled the teakettle with water, turned on the heat, then pulled out a chair and sat down to wait for

the water to boil. A cup of tea wasn't someone to talk to, but it might make her feel
warmer. When she was a very little girl, her
parents would sometimes let her join them
at the table, and it never mattered that
Angel's tea was more milk than anything.

Last night, after Jay had left, Angel had
gone to bed. Not to sleep, though. She
propped pillows behind her and sat waiting
for the phone to ring. She couldn't help
thinking that Jay had changed his mind, and
had stopped at Jody's. When he knew the
truth, the phone would ring, and it would be
all over for Angel. She didn't feel safe
enough to turn off the light until eleven-
thirty. It was too late for Jay or Jody to
phone.

Sipping her tea, Angel thought ahead to
when school would be out for the day. Would
she have a visitor? Visitors? Would anyone
call? Angel had never been a nail-biter, but
by noon, her nails on one hand were con-
siderably shorter.

What am I going to do?

There was a rehearsal that night, but it
made her feel weak even to think about it.
She could continue to play sick. Why not?

The suspense was doing a nasty job on her
nerves, Angel thought. If she didn't show up,
no one would have the song lyrics to study
before the next rehearsal. The set building
crew needed her experience and needed her
direction as well. She had many responsi-

bilities, and, besides, Mr. Damian would be lost if she didn't show up.

At least Angel would be able to find out what was going on, one way or another. She would judge by the way Jay and Jody acted toward her and each other on the stage and off. She *had* to know.

She watched TV for the rest of the afternoon, but didn't relax for a minute. The soaps rolled on, one into the other, and Angel couldn't have cared less, but *Ryan's Hope* and *General Hospital* were better than nothing.

Antsy, fidgety, climbing up and down imaginary walls, Angel somehow got through the afternoon until it was time for dinner.

It took every bit of stamina Angel had left to make a phone call and ask Mr. James if he would pick her up. Tania wasn't home, he said. She had gone with her mother to the mall but would be back before rehearsal time.

"What's new with you, Angel-cakes?" Mr. James asked heartily.

You wouldn't want to know, Angel thought. "Oh, you know, Mr. James, the play is the thing." It was an old joke of his and he sounded pleased that she remembered.

"Did Tania tell you that I've got a hay-wagon? Only problem is I can only have the use of it this Saturday night. You tell that pint-sized director not to schedule a rehearsal. I suppose I'm spoiling Tania's surprise. She probably wanted to tell you kids tonight."

"Oh, that's *great*, Mr. James. I'm really excited about it. We all are."

Another lie to add to her long list. She wasn't excited at all.

When Tania and Angel arrived at rehearsal, Jay and Jody were onstage with Mr. Damian. He appeared to be pointing out the marks where he wanted them to stand and move around each other during a particular scene. Angel couldn't tell which scene, but what was important was that they didn't look at each other, didn't laugh and make faces as they usually did. Both followed Mr. Damian's instructions, but Angel could see how stiff and awkward they were, and how hostile. Jody tossed a line of dialogue at Jay, and he tossed one back, looking over her head as he spoke. Angel's skin suddenly felt cold. Jay and Jody were enemies now. It was all her fault.

She turned away, relieved that Jay probably hadn't spoken to her again last night, but also filled with sadness. Angel knew that she couldn't help, couldn't tell them the truth now even if she could find the words. It was too complicated, and she had no idea how to explain it. She just wasn't sure of anything anymore.

During all the years that Angel had been telling stories . . . pretending, she had always been able to remember, keep things straight. She'd learned how important it was to keep her memory sharp and her stories consistent. Her memory was failing her now. What she'd said, what Jay said, what Jody had said on the phone were all balled up. It was like a tangled web.

Angel made her way to the back stage area and sat down at her old desk. Pushing papers around busily was the only thing she could think of to do.

"Angel — there you are. May I speak to you, please?"

"Sure, Mr. Damian. What about?"

"Let's go to the lounge. A little privacy there."

Angel followed the director, thinking all the way that he seemed troubled, thoughtful. She wondered what he had on his mind. She found out when she sat down in a chair opposite him.

His eyes looked like large black stones, and his mouth hard and thin. She felt the stirring of uneasiness.

"I'm very upset, Angel," he said. "I've already talked this over with my wife but she's as bewildered as I am. She knows what a monster I can be, but she thinks a lot of you kids. Angel, take a look at this."

Mr. Damian handed her a piece of lined notebook paper. She looked at it, noticed the date and the greeting — *Dear Mr. Damian.* She looked down to see who it was from and she froze. She was holding a letter to Mr. Damian from *Steve Ellis.*

"Should I read it, Mr. Damian?" Angel asked in what she hoped was an innocent voice.

"I wish you would, Angel. Then maybe you'll be able to figure this out."

She hoped that the director wasn't looking at her too closely; her hands were trembling.

Dear Mr. Damian:

I wasn't going to write this letter because I didn't think it would do any good, and I didn't want to inform on certain individuals. I guess you might say I was prepared to walk away with my pride while it was still in one piece and forget about drama club, *Grease*, and especially you, Mr. Damian.

I took my "so-so talent" elsewhere. I am now a member of Edgemont Community Players and I have the *lead* role of Jud in Bernard Slade's *Tribute*. Jud is a shy, rather *wimpy* character, so I think you'll agree that I fit the role perfectly. Jud also feels unloved, unappreciated, and he has a lot of problems with his father.

Mr. Damian, I never thought of you as a father but I did consider you my mentor, someone I could look up to and learn from. Plain and simple, it hurt a lot to know that you were talking about me behind my back, while encouraging me to my face.

Don't blame the one who repeated your remarks because she didn't know I was listening. This person is fine and sweet, and the hardest worker I know.

I know it wasn't her fault, and I feel sorry for her because she has to put up with you still.

I wish I could say that I don't have any hard feelings anymore, but it's not true. I am too confused.

Your former student
and former friend, Steve

Angel couldn't look up right away. Tears had welled up in her eyes and were threatening to spill over. A feeling of extreme fatigue settled over her, and, suddenly Steve's letter felt too heavy to hold.

"It's a sad letter, and a well written one," she said wearily. "He is smart."

Mr. Damian bent toward her, placing his hands on his knees. His dark eyes bored into hers. "Can you tell me what you know about this, Angel? Somehow, I can't think of another girl in our club who fits his description so perfectly."

There was nothing to say, nothing to do, she thought. She was backed into the corner and nothing she said was going to help. Mr. Damian's eyes were sad and knowing. He *knew* it was her. Poor Steve, though. He had suffered a lot and all because of her. He had written that he *liked* her. It was time to tell the truth.

She couldn't. The words stuck in her throat. Easily, sweetly, innocently, she said: "*Everyone* is a hard worker, and I guess, sweet, too. Name me one girl in our club who isn't nice? I'm flattered that you thought it was me, Mr. Damian."

"Flattered? Are you serious? Angel, you can't lie about this, and please, please, don't."

"Mr. Damian. Please." Angel was standing, trembling all over. She knew the tears were going to come at any second. "I don't know what you're talking about."

Mr. Damian sighed and leaned back. It was a large chair and he was a small man, and Angel thought he looked like a tired little boy.

"Angel Porter. My right hand. Indispensable, responsible, likeable, beautiful Angel. I never dreamed you had such acting ability." Back to normal, she thought, when she heard his sarcastic tone. He sighed again and got to his feet. He was a few inches shorter than Angel. "I want you to think this through tonight, Angel. Sleep on it, as they say. I want you to consider what someone has done to a classmate's life and self-image.

"Come on," he said. "We are leaving our cast in limbo. Forget about this for the next hour, please. Angel, you should know that the show . . . must go on." His face was a mass of crinkles and creases and he suddenly looked very old.

The director led the way back to the stage area. Angel lingered behind the door for a minute or two, and wiped the tears away with her sleeve. Her throat did feel sore now. When she finally got settled at her desk without anyone noticing, she looked up and saw Tania hurrying toward her *Not now,* she wanted to shout.

"What is going on tonight?" Tania asked impatiently, her hands framing her slim hips in the black corduroy jeans. "No one is saying anything, but I know when something's popping. Why isn't Jay talking to Jody and vice-versa?"

"Really, Tania? I haven't had time to notice anything."

"And what's with Mr. D? He looks like he just lost his best friend. What did he want to talk to you about? Anything to do with the letter from Steve Ellis?"

Angel almost choked. "What letter from Steve?" she asked carefully.

"I'm the one who made the special delivery," Tania said, posing. "Through rain and sleet and snow last study period on Friday."

"I don't know," Angel said weakly. *The only thing I do know is that Mr. Damian did lose a friend — two, in fact. Thanks to me.*

"If you find out anything, let me know, okay? Steve is a good kid and also — I'm nosy, in case you haven't noticed."

"I've noticed. Tania, someone's calling you. Aren't you supposed to be hoofing it with the Pink Ladies?"

"Right." Tania raised her voice. "Frenchy's coming, ladies. Angel, find out what's with J and J over there. Talk to you later."

Tania hadn't seemed to find anything

wrong with Angel's smile, voice, or dumb answers to her questions. Pretending to read a list, Angel looked from under her eyelashes and saw Jody standing in the wings forlornly, her posture poor, and her pink ballet slippers pointing outward. From her hand dangled her script, and she was staring over at Jay. He was sitting backward on a straight chair, his arms crossed, his back rigid under the black T-shirt. Angel couldn't see his face either, but she guessed that she wouldn't want to.

Several minutes later, when Angel spotted Jody heading her way, she ran, grabbing up a handful of papers as a cover. She ran through the stage door and down the hall to the girls' room. She locked herself in a booth, and leaned against the gray steel partition. It was cool, and she was hot. Burning deep inside was a shame so deep that it stunned her. Her mouth dropped open and a huge sob escaped, an ugly, retching sound. The sound of it frightened her, and she left the booth quickly and stood at the row of sinks, not daring to meet her own eyes.

Look what you've done, Angel. Just look what you've done.

They were thoughts she knew, but they echoed eerily in her head. She couldn't look. She turned and left the tiled room and loitered in the dim hall. Rehearsal would be over shortly. Everyone would be leaving, which meant she was going to have to face them: Tania, Jody, and Jay.

It suddenly occurred to her that Jay hadn't spoken to her either. When she arrived he had been working with Jody and Mr. Damian. Then she'd gone to the lounge with the director. Jay was sitting alone when Tania was questioning her.

He's not ignoring me, Angel thought. *He just hasn't had a chance to talk to me. As soon as rehearsal ends, he'll come looking for me. He always does, and he's never very attentive when he's concentrating on his role.*

I can't lose Jay. I just can't. I love him.

She knew she couldn't wait around to find out if he still loved her. She walked down the hall to the pay phone and dialed her home number.

"Dad, could you pick me up at school? Please? I feel so sick. Faint, dizzy, horrible."

"Well, sure," Dad said. "Since you're so sick."

"Were you already in bed, Dad?" Angel asked guiltily.

"No. We stayed up very late tonight, your mother and me." He laughed. Big joke, Angel thought hopelessly. Goody for them.

She hadn't been lying. She did feel faint, dizzy, and horrible. On the way out of Edgemont High, Angel wondered if anyone would miss her.

Thirteen

Angel went to school the next morning feeling as if she were walking to her own execution. No one was waiting at the corner for her, but it could have been because she was too early.

She didn't see anyone before the first bell, and when she left home room for the first period English, she kept her head down as she walked along the carpeted hall.

She had to look up unless she wanted to crash. Someone was blocking her path. It was Jay. Angel recognized the striped shirt. It was the one he'd worn that first day when she had bumped into him.

"Hi, Jay," she said tentatively, searching his face for clues. It looked like a papier-mâché mask, she thought. Stiff and hard and unsmiling. He stood there, staring down at her, and his hazel eyes were dark green and dull.

"I shouldn't even bother," he said finally. "Someone has to, though. Jody's in bad shape right now, so I said I would . . . talk to you."

"Yes?" Angel didn't know what else to say. She wasn't going to bite any more than that. Jay had dangled the bait and Angel knew she was supposed to ask why her friend wasn't in good shape.

"Why do you do it?" he asked. "Not just this latest bag of tricks. You've been doing it all along, haven't you? Tania, Jody, and I have been comparing notes and we've figured out that you've been lying for a long time. We've been remembering all these things that you got us to believe."

Angel met his eyes for the first time. It was too much . . . *comparing notes . . . talking about her.* The idea hurt so much. Angel wondered if she could stand here any longer when it hurt so much inside. "Jay, don't. Don't say these things. You really don't know what —"

He laughed harshly. "It's kind of funny, actually, in a rotten kind of way. I fell for it . . . boy, did I ever. It's still hard to believe. I mean, Angel with the innocent baby blues, the gorgeous face. What a jerk I've been."

"No, Jay. You haven't been. You just know what Jody and Tania are telling you. They really don't know me. No one does. Everyone just sees what they want to see, thinks what they want to think about me. It's not fair — I can't stand it anymore."

Angel put her hands over her face but the tears dripped through her fingers. She didn't even care who saw her now.

"*It's not fair?*" Jay's voice was incredulous. "Was it *fair* what you did to Steve, Angel? Yeah, we know about that, too, and it's a lot worse than what you did to Jody and me. How can you sleep at night?"

"How do you know about Steve? What did Mr. Damian tell you?" Angel forced the words out between sobs. It was now or never, she thought. Maybe she could save herself if she really tried. It was the director's word against hers.

Jay's voice was low but it carried such contempt that Angel flinched.

"It's one thing to claim you've read fifteen books when the author has only one to her name. It's another thing to try to ruin friendships, and make up vicious lies about someone. What did Steve Ellis ever do to you? What did Jody ever do except be a good friend? You are the pits, you know that? I can't stand your face anymore. *Angel —* what a joke you are."

Jay had gone. Angel hadn't heard him walk away because she'd been crying too hard. She couldn't remember ever crying so painfully, the sobs tearing out of her with such wrenching force. A joke . . . *I'm a joke,* she thought despairingly. *Jay hates me . . . everyone hates me.*

What was she going to do?

Stumbling into the girls' room, Angel turned on the cold water, and leaning over the sink, cupped her hands and bathed her hot face. It took a long time until she felt calm enough to dry her face with a paper towel, and longer still before she could open her eyes and look at herself in the mirror.

It was a relief somehow to see that she didn't look pretty at all. Her skin was dull and sallow, she thought, and her eyelids were red and puffy. Her mouth wouldn't stay still; she pressed her lips together hard to try and stop them from quivering. Her hair was wet around her face and matted in places. Her eyes, usually a soft pastel blue, looked flat gray and the whites around them were bloodshot.

It was fitting that she looked so ugly, she thought. The outside finally matched the inside. She'd been so ugly all along. She imagined that her friends — her *ex*-friends — would call her a few appropriate names among themselves. Jay said she was a joke. They would refer to her, maybe, as "that awful Angel."

She knew it was too late for her. Too late to try and make amends. She was sure Jody and Tania wanted nothing to do with her anymore.

She didn't know how she did it, when she thought about it later, but Angel had made it to every class. It was the numbness that helped, she thought, the feeling of being a robot. She'd walked to and from class, to the lunchroom, and finally, home, all on automatic pilot. At lunch, she avoided the area where she usually sat with Jay, Jody, and Tania, and ate a cheeseburger and fries alone at an almost-empty table in the corner.

It was only Tuesday, she thought, lying flat on her bed. She wondered dully how she would make it to Friday. How could she miss school? Someone in the school office would call home, and, maybe question her mother about Angel's absences.

And the hayride was planned for Saturday night. She could just forget about that.

Rehearsals . . . Mr. Damian . . . what was she going to do?

Angel was so quiet at dinner, her parents actually noticed. She almost choked on her broccoli when her mother said brightly, "Is something the matter, honey? You haven't said a word. Jack, when's the last time we heard our Angel tell one of her fascinating stories? Honey, really, you're not still sick, are you?"

"No, Mom — just tired." She *did* feel sick. She just wanted to sleep and not think about anything.

The doorbell rang. Her father jumped up and ran to answer the door before Angel could move.

Her mother got up, too. "It's Ed and Dot Miller. They're bringing some new friends of theirs over to meet us and play cards."

"Go ahead, Mom," Angel said quickly. "Don't worry about the dishes. I'll do them and straighten up."

Mom flashed her a grateful smile. "You're a wonderful girl, do you know that?"

Angel looked away. "Mmmmm," she said to satisfy her mother. "Thanks."

Wonderful daughter — another joke. She couldn't stop the tears then, and she didn't even bother to wipe them away. The slow tears had trickled down her cheeks, but they had stopped, and where they'd dried, her skin itched liked crazy. She was rubbing at her face when her parents ushered four people into the kitchen. Angel saw her mother looking at her critically before she smiled and became the gracious hostess again.

"This is our Angel," Dad said proudly. "The living, breathing version. Angel, they loved your portrait. Honey, meet Josh and Meg Bennet. They're new in town. Of course, you know Ed and Dot."

Angel managed to be polite, and she forced a smile on her face, knowing her mother wasn't too happy with her strained, tear-streaked child. Angel was very glad when they all went into the family room.

Angel spent the night watching television. She borrowed the portable TV from her parents' bedroom, and sat until eleven o'clock watching one program after another. It helped her not to think. During commercials though, the thoughts about Jay and Jody returned to torment her. She had to get up and pace around her room until the TV show began again. When she turned off the light, it was as if a demon inside her was taking great pleasure in unreeling a long line of memories and images that would hurt the most. Jody, pert and smiling, telling her that she was always there for her. Jay, his arms around her, saying, "I think I love you, Angel." Tania, phoning her as soon as she returned from Staten Island every Sunday night. "I had to call you, Angel. You always know exactly what I mean."

Angel had been Tania's first friend. Tania had come to Edgemont, and to school that first day, with a chip on her shoulder. Tania told her later that she was simply terrified. Angel had seen through the defensive, tough pose, and had invited her to sit at their table in the cafeteria. Tania had been her loyal supporter, her biggest fan. "Angel is the best," she told anyone who would listen.

Finally, the demon (who looked suspiciously like Pinocchio) took pity on her, and she slept.

In the morning she got ready for school. It would be another day of torture, forcing herself to act normal. She wasn't sure she could make it, but she did. Lonesome and sad weren't strong enough words to describe how she felt inside. If she passed Jody or Jay in the hall, they ignored her, looked past her to a spot on the wall.

On Wednesday night she asked her mother for a ride to rehearsal. She made up the excuse that she had to be there before Tania or Jody. At rehearsal she went around doing what she had to do, but when Mr. Damian approached and looked at her questioningly, Angel told him calmly, "Please don't ask me anything. Just leave me alone."

He backed off silently, but Angel caught

the worried look . . . and the disgust. She had figured out that the director had talked to Jody or Tania, or both. They'd told him that it was Angel who said the things that sent Steve running into the darkness. They all knew now that she had passed off the remarks as Mr. Damian's. What else was there to say about it? The only thing that was keeping Angel going was her work. For the past few days, at home, at school, she had attacked everything with a cold passion — finishing both end tables, doing her homework, making copies of the lyrics, retyping her lists, and completing a pen-and-ink sketch for the play program. Marla Ryan was in charge of putting the pages in proper booklet form and writing the short bios for the stars, the cast of characters, and the crew.

Angel wasn't going to quit, she'd decided. She couldn't face the prospect of being completely cut off and alone. It wasn't going to be easy, but she was determined to see the play through to the end. It was punishment, though. When Angel got home Wednesday night, she went straight up to bed and cried herself to sleep.

Friday night rehearsal was the worst. Angel was in the back, quietly painting a lifeguard's stand with white paint. She looked up to see Tania standing there looking at her thoughtfully. Angel was silent, and she tried to squelch the tiny leap of hope. What did Tania want, anyway?

"I just want to know if it's true," she said quietly. "I keep thinking about you. . . . I keep thinking it's all a mistake. I know you, Angel. I thought I did. Why? Just tell me, okay?"

Angel looked up into the suffering face. Tania looked so strange, she thought, then realized it was because her warm brown skin and features were almost always set in lines of laughing, good-nature. Now she looked like a totally different person, and Angel didn't know what to say to her.

"It's not a mistake, Tania. All I can say is . . . I'm sorry. I didn't mean to hurt anyone, though. . . . I just . . ." Angel's voice trailed off and she turned her head away. "That's all . . . I guess," she said after Tania didn't move. "Could you just . . . go away, please?"

If Tania didn't move fast, Angel thought, she was going to have a sobbing, blubbering angel on her hands. A joke . . . she was a joke. "Please?"

Angel heard her friend move away but it was a long time before Angel's eyes were clear enough to look up. When she did, she saw Jody, Tania, and Jay standing to one side of the stage watching Mr. Damian demonstrate a series of dance steps.

Her heart skipped a beat, or at least that's what it felt like as she watched her friends standing together, and realized with horrible finality that they were going to be standing together against her from now on. She would never be part of them again; their lives wouldn't include her. After enough time had gone by, they probably wouldn't even think of her. Indifferent instead of disgusted, where Angel Porter was concerned.

Angel got through Saturday by cleaning her room of sawdust and raking the yard until late afternoon. The air was rich with the smell of wet, rotting leaves, and the ground was hard and already winter-cold beneath her sneakered feet. By four-thirty she was finished, and so physically exhausted that she dozed off in her jacket when she sat down in front of the fire.

"Wake up, Angel. As a reward for being such a hard worker today, your mother and I are taking you out to dinner. Nothing fancy, so you only have to change your shirt and jacket, and fix your face. We're very hungry, so please hurry."

Her parents wouldn't take no for an answer, so, grudgingly, Angel got ready, wishing that they would just go out by themselves as usual, and leave her alone.

York Steak House at the mall wasn't too crowded, and Angel was grateful for the dim lighting and the high-backed booths. She ate her dinner without enthusiasm, and gave only short answers when her parents asked her questions. For once she was glad that they had little trouble carrying the conversation by themselves. Angel was glad when they finished their coffee and pie, and it was time to leave.

She chose to sit on a bench by herself while they browsed in the bookstore. Why should she go in and be reminded of her stupid lie about Marietta Tindale? In a miserable mood, Angel sat and waited, wishing her parents would hurry up and take her home. She wanted to go to sleep early so she wouldn't have to think about this particular Saturday night.

Later, when she was in bed, Angel wondered if there really was such a thing as coincidence. It had to be something more than coincidence that on the way home from the mall, her father managed to get behind a large, hay-filled wagon. He hadn't really had to follow it like that, so slowly and relentlessly, until it turned onto Pine Avenue.

Her mother had been confused at first, but after a moment, she'd put two and two together. "Angel, aren't those your friends in that haywagon? Why aren't you with them? I think you'd better tell me what's going on."

Angel had stared ahead at the swaying wagon, at the lanterns that glowed all around the base, at a silhouette of a person with a guitar, and she hadn't said a word.

Even when both parents ganged up on her and ordered her to tell them the truth, she didn't — couldn't — tell them.

Tell them the truth? Angel rolled over and buried her head under her pillow. What was the difference, she wondered. And, anyway, why start now?

*F*ourteen

Two more weeks passed and suddenly it was the first of December and the night of dress rehearsal. Angel was both glad and worried sick that the play was almost over and done with. She was glad because she knew it was impossible to continue the awkward role she had to play at rehearsals and at school. She hadn't made any move to apologize to Jody, but she thought about it constantly. She was worried about what she would do after the play was over. If she thought she was lonesome and miserable now, how would she feel afterward? Angel tried not to think about it, or look ahead too far.

The dress rehearsal would begin immediately after school, Mr. Damian had said. They would do well to bring a couple of sandwiches from home because he would keep them prisoner until everything was perfect. Angel knew from experience how impossible that goal was; dress rehearsals were, traditionally, chaotic. Everything always went wrong. No one in the cast would be able to sleep that night. They wouldn't believe that the play would be anything but disaster. Oh, a few of the old-timers like Jody and Tania would know everything would turn out all right, Angel thought. She was sure that Jay would be a total nervous wreck. He had been one at the last few rehearsals. His stagefright was worse than Angel had ever seen, but she had to watch from the sidelines and only fantasize about being able to comfort him. Too bad he wasn't hers anymore, she'd thought more than once.

Angel wasn't happy, but in a way, she had gotten used to feeling like an outcast, and in a way, almost relished it because she knew she deserved it. Other members of the cast weren't rude to her, or anything like that. They just kept out of her way as much as possible.

She was the first one to reach the auditorium after school. She even beat the custodian, Mr. Moran. He greeted her with a wave and a smile. He was a nice man, Angel thought, and no one ever paid the slightest attention to him. For that reason, she suddenly walked over and chatted with him for a few minutes. He was friendly and seemed pleased that she was, too. She knew exactly how he felt.

The stage was dark except for one dim light in back over her desk. She didn't want to go back there and sit alone, so instead, she sat down on the edge of the stage, and opened the brown paper bag. She'd spent the lunch period at the media center, because it was just too terrible sitting by herself in the cafeteria. She was hungry. She was also glad that she'd thought to bring more than one sandwich. The tuna she'd mixed that morning before school was just the right amount for three sandwiches, and rather than putting the mix back in the refrigerator, she'd made the extra sandwich. She could eat two now, and save one for later.

"Something's pretty fishy around here."

Angel strained to see who was speaking in the almost dark auditorium. In his black outfit, Mr. Damian was invisible until he reached the stage. Angel gulped. Except for things pertaining to the production, they hadn't spoken since that time in the lounge.

"You can smell tuna way back there?" she asked, hoping she sounded casual.

"When you're as hungry as I am, you can. I missed lunch."

He reached up, and Angel understood that he wanted her to help him up on the stage. He was so light, Angel pulled him up easily. "Here," she said, handing him a baggie-wrapped sandwich. "I can take a hint." She didn't know she was going to add, "Just don't ever go on a three-day fast, Mr. Damian."

He squinted at her, and she realized that he had no idea what she meant. "Me? Fast? You want me to disappear?"

"No, I don't," she said seriously. He nodded, but he couldn't talk with a mouthful of tuna sandwich. "It was just a private joke.

From me to me. Not funny."

"The past few weeks haven't been funny for you either, have they, Angel?"

She shook her head. "You can say that again. Don't feel bad for me, though. You *know* I deserve it. May I ask you something?

He was chewing again, but he nodded.

"What did you do about Steve Ellis? Did you write him back?"

"Mmph . . . I . . . talked . . . mmph . . . to him, instead. He's okay now."

"Oh," she said, and sighed. "But what does he think of me now? Not so sweet, huh?"

"If you feel like it, have a heart-to-heart with him sometime."

Angel was silent. She kept rolling the brown paper bag like a ball in her hands. Finally, she said, "Thanks, Mr. Damian. I'll talk to him. I promise."

"Just stop thinking that you're the worst person in the whole world," he said, jumping up and walking across the stage to the wings and the light switches. "If you want to compare bad characters, I could beat you by a mile and twenty years."

"Oh, no, Mr. Damian. I'm the —"

"You're my assistant, aren't you? Let's get started here. No more talk until after dress rehearsal, please. I can't take it." He was back to his grouchy, normal self, Angel thought, glad that the darkness hid her smile. It wouldn't do if she looked grateful, she knew. Mr. Damian would hate it.

A few at a time, looking jittery, the members of the cast trailed into the auditorium and up on the stage. There were self-conscious remarks and expressions as they looked at each other in full fifties dress. Angel thought that Jay looked fabulous in the black leather jacket, black pants, and white T-shirt. She thought he out-Travolta-ed John by a wide margin.

Jody looked adorable, too, in her first act outfit. At the beginning of the play Sandy shows up for her first date with Danny in a fluffy, ruffled dress. She's a real goody-two-shoes, and Danny likes her a lot but doesn't think he's her type. Angel remembered the pink ruffled dress very well. Jody had worn it to her eighth grade graduation and despised it. She'd even offered it to Angel because she thought it would look better on her.

The memory was strong and so was her feeling for Jody as Angel watched her smile and cross the stage, then stick out her tongue playfully at a laughing Danny Zuko. Jody looked really pretty, Angel thought. Maybe it was the blond, ponytailed wig and the padded bra. Realizing what she'd just thought, Angel turned and hurried back to the curtained backstage. She was ashamed of herself again. She had hated that kind of judgment, and now she was doing it, too.

"All right, cast . . . everybody in their places. Lighting ready up there? Frenchy . . . tie your shoelace. Get ready to give me your best show, gang. I think I deserve it . . .

putting up with all of you lughead klutzes." His scowl was certainly a fake one, and Angel felt a sudden affection for the hard-working director. He was mostly bark and very little bite, she thought.

Lighting wasn't ready. They kept everyone waiting for ten minutes while they adjusted the spots and fiddled with the footlights. Mr. Damian was beginning to quiver with anxiety.

It got worse. No one knew their lines. Even Jody went to pieces because she couldn't remember the lyrics to "Danny, My Love." Jay slipped on a stray sheet of script and almost fell. Mr. Damian picked up the offending paper and accused the entire cast of trying to sabotage his efforts. He went around the stage like a maniac waving the single page in everyone's face and asking if they knew their lines, or if not, maybe they wanted their "crib-sheet" back. He was a tyrant — a steaming, glaring, half-out-of-his-mind wreck. Angel knew he was enjoying himself.

It was during the beach scene that Angel first caught Jody looking at her. It wasn't a hostile glance, Angel thought, but it wasn't friendly either. Anyway, she couldn't worry about it. She was goofing up a little, too. She'd misplaced the beachball, and also the stagehands hadn't bothered to put up the hot dog stand set.

And then she caught Jay doing it, too. *What were they looking at?* Even though she knew it was silly, Angel checked to see if all her buttons were buttoned, and her zipper zipped. When act one ended, she had to supervise the setting up of the Chevy, and she didn't have time to worry about Jay. *He probably just doesn't like having me watch him fall apart,* she thought. *I'm his enemy now, and Jody's, too, I guess.*

Act two wasn't too bad. Mr. Damian had a rest. Jody was singing well, and Angel got tears in eyes when she sang her part of "Summer Lovin'." The Pink Ladies were on one side of the stage, and the T-Birds, macho and greasily handsome, were on the other. Angel got that special excitement watching them, and knew that this number was going to be a big hit with the audience. Mr. Damian once told her that she would make a good director because of that sixth sense that told her what would work in the action, and what wouldn't.

At the end of act two, Mr. Damian called a break.

"Cast, empty your lunchbags, man those thermos bottles. I want you in your best shape for act three. Twenty minutes, and you should bless me for that. It was going to be five."

Angel watched everyone disappear from the stage, but she lingered in the wings, imagining that there was a full house beyond the footlights. She loved this . . . all the excitement and the hard work. The beginning of a production was as important as the ending, she thought. She didn't like to think about the promise she'd made to herself, to quit drama club after *Grease*. For the remainder of this school year, and all through the next, Angel wouldn't have anything to belong to.

The sadness lifted a little when she looked at the bright red, battered car. Even better, Mr. James' name would appear in large letters on the program. Angel had insisted on that, although Marla Ryan protested that the large print was "horsey," a printer's way of saying "overdone, overlarge, and just plain too much." So what? Mr. Harold James was going to see his acknowledgment without having to put on his reading glasses, Angel thought now.

She didn't really have much to do. And she was very thirsty, but she was afraid to go into the lounge. What if Jody and Jay were there?

A few minutes later, she was too thirsty to care. She headed for the lounge, with two quarters ready in her hand. If they were there, she'd get in and right out again. She wouldn't even look at them.

Everyone was in the lounge. Angel didn't take the time to look for anyone special. But just her luck, when she dropped her change into the slot, and pressed the Coke lever, nothing happened. She pressed the coin return button — nothing! She banged lightly on the big machine — nothing! She banged harder, angry and embarrassed — still nothing!

"Are you sure you put two quarters in?" a voice behind her asked. Angel turned, frowning. Her eyes got very wide.

"Jay!"

He was smiling at her but looked very serious at the same time.

"Jay, you're smiling at me. Don't you hate me?"

He shook his head, and his vaselined hair came slightly unstuck. He would need help redoing his pompadour, she thought. "I did hate you, Angel. Past tense. You did some terrible things and now we have to talk. There must be some reason why you acted the way you did."

She sat down on the arm of the old couch, and listened as he told her how he had talked things over with Jody yesterday, and they decided maybe that they'd been too hard on her.

"Jody said it hurt her to see you so alone all the time. She said that you're pretty lonely at home, too. We decided you had guts to keep on with the play, and all."

"I thought I could force my mother and father to pay attention to me," Angel said. "I tried to do it with stories, which later weren't stories at all, but lies, more and more of them. They're not bad people, Jay, they're just not very good parents — 'good' by *my* idea of what parents should be. I guess no one really has perfect parents." She saw his face. "Oh, Jay — I'm sorry, I didn't mean you."

She saw his smile and knew she hadn't spoiled it. His smile told her that he was a lot more comfortable with his mother's disease than he had been.

"We have a lot to talk about, Angel . . . and we will."

Then break was over. Jay didn't walk with her; he ran ahead and in a few minutes, Angel saw that he was a wreck again, stage-frightened from head to toe.

She was still in a state of shock. Not only had he spoken to her, he had been friendly. He seemed a little guarded though. Angel spotted Jody talking to Jay, and she saw her head fall back and her mouth open. She was laughing — hard. Angel felt a shiver of fear and doubt. *What if they were laughing at her?*

It could be, she thought. *All a set-up. An ugly joke on Angel Porter.*

The doubt faded, and Angel could think clearly again. It wasn't something either of them would do — or could do. They weren't . . . sneaky. They didn't treat people that way. Angel wondered for a moment if Jay or Jody had ever lied. Or Tania. Funny, they probably had once or twice, now that she thought of it. Maybe not lied but exaggerated and embroidered for better effect.

Act three didn't allow time for thinking. Angel was busy, coaching, prompting, fixing a torn costume, sliding sets on and off stage with her crew. She was perspiring heavily when the curtain went down.

And up again. And down. Mr. Damian was wild; something was wrong with the pulley. Angel had to stay to calm him down and put things away, and by the time she was ready to call home for a ride, everyone had already gone home.

Mr. Damian was walking. She decided to join him. She knew he lived three streets past her in a blue split-level. He seemed happy for the company.

"So how did you think it went tonight?" he asked.

"Just right," she said gaily. "Awfuulll."

"Let's hope it's not awwwwfuuullll tomorrow night, Angel."

She laughed. "You sounded just like a frog."

In the fluorescent lights outside the school building, he kind of looked like one, too, she thought.

"Well, I was a prince once," he said sadly. "And then my wife went and kissed me." He sighed tragically. "You just can't win in this life, Angel."

She glanced at him sideways as they walked together. "Are you sure about that, Mr. D?"

He shook his head. "Not sure at all. Try it, Angel. It's about time you started winning."

He was absolutely right, Angel decided, after she turned down her street and waved good-bye. And she was going to start immediately.

Fifteen

The velvet stage curtains were soft and cool against her arm. At four that afternoon, Angel had started checking her lists again, and, now, five minutes before curtain, everything and everyone was ready. She dearly hoped so anyway. As usual, just before the play was about to begin, Mr. Damian in a sharply tailored gray suit, was calm and peaceful. Looking at him, standing across the stage in the wings, Angel thought that no one would ever guess he could be a monster.

Looks are deceiving, though. If her parents chose to care more about her looks than her person, that was their loss. She had finally decided that she could live with the fact that they loved each other best. It made sense in a way. Their love for each other *had* come first. She came — was born — after that fact.

"What do you think, Angel. Is it going to be our best show, or what?"

Angel turned sharply and saw Jody standing beside her. In her blond wig and goody-two-shoes dress, she looked innocently beautiful. A fluffy angel.

"The best," Angel said breathlessly. It was what she'd wished for so hard, that Jody would forgive her. Maybe just by coming to stand beside her, and asking a casual question, she was doing just that. "Jody, you poor thing, you almost look like me in that wig." It would be great if they could laugh together. Angel thought that she would give anything to make her friend laugh.

"Thanks," Jody said primly. "I thought so, too." Suddenly, she *was* laughing. "I don't think Jay sees the resemblance. You're the only angel in *his* life."

Angel moved closer, and tried to see if Jody was serious. She had to look into her eyes . . . had to know if she was lying or telling the truth.

"Jody, are you . . . ? Angel closed her mouth. She couldn't ask her that. Jody would never lie. She would empathize — know what Angel was feeling. She always had.

"One minute to curtain, folks!" The rasping call wasn't loud but Angel knew that everyone had heard it. You could hear a pin drop.

"I think I'm going to throw up." It was Jay, coming to stand between Jody and Angel. "I'm going to blow it. I can feel it. I can't remember my first line."

"You'll be fine," Angel whispered. "Break a leg."

Angel saw him jump back and even in the dim light she saw the look of horror on his face. Jody saw it, too, and clapped a hand over her mouth to keep from laughing. When she was in control again, Jody said: "Take it easy. Angel wasn't being nasty. It's show biz for 'good luck.' Didn't you know that?"

"I'm new at this," Jay said, and cleared his throat nervously.

Peeking through the curtain, Angel watched as the house lights went down and the baby spot light up where Danny would stand when the curtain opened.

"I have to go now . . . Angel." She barely felt the kiss, it was so quick. He walked on-stage in his black leather jacket and his slick head held high. He was going to be great as Danny, she thought, the sixth sense coming to her stronger than ever before. "As Jay, he isn't bad either," she said out loud. She felt Jody's arm slip around her waist and squeeze.

"You aren't bad either, Angel. Don't worry any more. We love you."

"I'm so sorry, Jody. I don't know if you can believe me."

The curtain was going up now, and Angel held her breath.

"I do believe you. From this moment on."

From that moment on, Angel knew it would all be fine. They would be friends again — Jay, Jody, Tania, and Angel.

They were the ones she wanted. Best of all, they wanted her, too.

Are you a SUNFIRE® girl?

Find out! Order now!

Read all about the fascinating young women who lived and loved during America's most turbulent times!
